HOLLY BOUGH COTTAGE

Holiday Cottage Series Book Two

CINDY GUNDERSON

Button Press

FOREWORD

The Holiday Cottages are magical places where those who come to Sprucewood, CO to 'get away' find themselves and their hopes renewed, relationships kindled, and dreams coming true. Read the twelve Holiday Cottage books in this series...

L iv kicked her sandals off and picked them up, allowing her feet to sink into the powdery white sand. She hadn't been home long enough to take this view for granted like she used to. She knew she'd eventually settle back into a routine, but for now, the deep oranges and reds of the sunset bouncing off the waves was pure magic.

Liv took a deep breath. The cool ocean air filled her lungs and momentarily eased the tightness in her chest. She walked toward the water and tossed her flip-flops on the beach, laying her handbag and sunglasses next to them. She pulled her cardigan closed across her chest, allowing it to insulate her body slightly from the breeze as she dipped her toes in the surf.

Closing her eyes, Liv sucked in a breath as the frigid water washed gently over the tops of her feet. Reaching into the pocket of her linen shorts, she pulled out a hair elastic and quickly wrapped her long, blond hair into a bun to keep it out of her eyes. Then, wriggling her toes in the soft sand, she attempted to process the events that led to her standing on this very beach. The beach she grew up on. The beach she thought she'd left behind for good.

Nobody enjoys having to come crawling back to their parents in their late twenties, but especially not when said parents had predicted it in the first place. Thankfully, she'd found a rental in town she could afford, so at least she didn't need to crash in her old bedroom. Still. It irked her that they'd been right about any part of it. She hadn't been able to handle New York City, just like they said. And she hadn't been able to handle Connor.

When goosebumps started to lift on her skin, she walked back to her belongings and reluctantly picked them up, then made her way along the weathered wooden planks to the parking lot.

"Hey, Mom," Liv said, answering the phone just moments after walking inside and shutting her front door.

"How are you?" her mother asked.

"Good. Just got back from the beach."

"A little cold, don't you think?"

"It wasn't too bad," Liv said, brushing the sand from the sides of her feet and walking to the couch.

"Do you feel settled?"

Liv laughed. "It's only been a week. No, definitely not settled. But I do have a clear path from the living room to the kitchen."

"Well, that's something," her mother said. "I bet you're loving this weather compared to New York, at least?"

"It's pleasant," Liv agreed but cringed internally. She loved everything about New York over the holidays. It wasn't until February that she missed the Panhandle.

"He hasn't called you, has he?" Liv's mother asked, her voice tense.

"No, Mom," Liv sighed. "Everything was finalized the week after Thanksgiving, remember? That's why I had to wait 'till then to—"

"I know, I know," she cut in. "I just still can't believe—"

"You and me both, Mom," Liv sighed, cutting her comment short. She had no desire to rehash Connor's actions with her mother. Again. "I need to get some dinner," she said. "I'll see you tomorrow?"

"Are you coming out to help Dad with the cabbages and brussel sprouts?"

"That's the plan," Liv said. "How long do you think it'll take?"

"Not long. He didn't plant much this year. We're getting old enough that he's satisfied with a few boxes to take to the market on Saturday. Ooh!" she exclaimed. "I promised your father I'd ask about your Christmas plans. Will you be joining us? Tamara, Joe, and the kids are coming out on the 21st. They'll be staying with us through the New Year, I think."

Liv groaned internally. Though they were only three years apart, her older sister had been married for ten years and had four children to show for it.

"I'm not sure, Mom. I'm still figuring out my work situation. I have a few clients I need to touch base with before I can commit."

"You really think they're going to make you fly back to New York that close to Christmas?"

"Nobody knows I'm *not* in New York, remember? Normally I'd be working right up until Christmas Eve. You wouldn't believe the number of people who want to hire out an emergency redesign right before they host a holiday dinner."

"But don't you have a team for that?"

"Yes, Mom. I just don't know yet. I'll get back to you as soon as I can, okay?"

"Alright," her mother sighed, defeated for the moment. "See you in the morning."

"Love you," Liv said.

"Love you, too, honey."

L iv didn't waste any time. The second the phone call with her mother ended, she pulled her laptop out from under the couch, lifted the screen, and immediately began searching. Was she callous for purposefully trying to avoid a family Christmas dinner? Probably. But right now, she didn't care.

Even when she and Connor were married, it was painful to spend time with Tamara and Joe. Their marriage was clearly one built on mutual respect, and hers...was clearly not. She loved her sister, but she would rather poke her own eyes out than have to spend a week watching them snuggle on the couch, kiss under the mistletoe her mother always hung in the entryway, or laugh while they played tag with their kids in the backyard.

Thinking about it made her stomach turn. No. She needed to be far, far away from that this year. Preferably far away from *all* humans. There had to be some AirBnB where she could hole up, drink hot cocoa by the fire, and watch sappy Christmas movies to her heart's delight. And possibly do some work. There was that.

Liv thought for a moment as she stared at the search bar. 'Where are you going?' it asked. Wasn't that the million-dollar question? She began to type 'California,' but then quickly deleted it. She had beaches here. If she was going to travel for Christmas, she might as well go big.

She typed 'Colorado,' filled out her flexible dates of December 13-27th, and hit enter. A map materialized in front of her with a scroll bar along the right showing gorgeous homes and cabins available to rent. Clicking on 'price,' she filtered the results, and immediately a listing caught her eye. Holiday Cottages for rent in Sprucewood—near Golden, whatever that meant. Besides looking a little like one of those perpetual holiday stores had thrown up all over the interior, the place looked idyllic. Individual cottages on a Christmas tree farm, fireplace, full kitchen, excellent ratings—'a cozy cabin to truly get away from it all.'

She forced herself to peruse a few other listings—just in case there was a better option or a tempting deal—but after a few minutes, she was convinced the Holiday Cottages were exactly what she needed. Was she actually going to do this? Just take off for two weeks and spend Christmas alone? Her finger hesitated over the 'book now' button. How would she explain this to her family?

Emotion bubbled up in her chest as an image of her family on Christmas Day flashed through her mind. Their smiling faces, the kids running around the kitchen as they attempted to cook dinner. The questions about Connor—about what she planned to do next...

She clicked the button and hastily entered her credit card information before her guilt could take hold and force her to change her mind.

. . .

"I feel like Mom underestimated the amount of harvesting we'd be doing today," Liv complained the next morning, walking down the rows of their small family farm.

"Are you surprised?" her dad chuckled.

"No," she laughed.

"I don't think it'll take us long. If you want, we could have a competition like we did when you were little. That always made the time pass a little faster."

Liv jumped as 'Yellow Submarine' by the Beatles began playing in her back pocket. She quickly pulled out her phone and sent it to voicemail.

"Who was that?" her dad asked, raising an eyebrow.

"Matt, from work."

"Yellow submarine?"

Liv grinned. "It's an inside joke." She silenced her phone and slipped it back into the pocket of her jeans.

"When *was* the last time I helped with a harvest?" she asked, kicking a rock out of her way.

"Before everything with..." her dad started, then cleared his throat.

"Right," Liv pursed her lips, placing her hands on her hips. "Well, I'm glad to be here now. And I don't think we need to create a competition. Hand me a knife, old man."

Her father carefully pulled two sharp blades from his belt and gently handed one to her. Liv watched as he bent over, taking his time getting down to the level of the first cabbage plant in the row. She followed suit, leaning over and using the knife to remove the dense, green head from the leafy plant.

"How much longer do you think you'll be doing this?" she asked.

"I figure it will take us until just before lunch," he answered.

"No," Liv laughed. "I mean, how long you'll be gardening and selling produce at the market."

"I know, just teasing," he said, placing another head in the canvas sack on the ground next to him. "I don't know, honestly. Until it gets boring?"

"No desire for a real retirement?"

"Not if it involves sitting around and doing nothing."

Liv smiled. She wouldn't expect anything less from her dad, who, from the time she could remember, was always conjuring up new and exciting ways to use his time. Having a hobby that kept him close to home was probably a significant improvement from the activities he'd chosen in the past. At least in her mother's eyes.

"So you won't be joining us for Christmas?" her dad asked softly.

"She told you?"

"She did."

"That's unfortunate. I didn't think you two had crossed paths after I broke her heart with the news," Liv said, grunting as she struggled with a particularly stubborn plant.

"We communicate telepathically at this point. That's what happens when you've been married for forty years."

"Thirty-nine," Liv quipped, turning just in time to see her father chuckle.

"Close enough."

"I don't know, Dad. I don't think you get to claim the big 4-0 without actually earning it."

"You're avoiding my question."

"Is it working?"

"Not in the least," he laughed.

Liv sighed. "I have a lot of work to do, and I know that once Tamara gets here, I'm going to get pressured into doing family stuff every day, which—don't get me wrong, is awesome—but I won't be able to get everything done. And I'll be getting back on the twenty-seventh, so I can still see everyone for a few days before they head home."

Her dad was silent, slowly slicing and dropping cabbage into his bag behind her.

"No comment?" she asked.

"I didn't think you were finished," he said gently.

Liv stood up and turned to face him.

"You can give that excuse to your mom, but I'm not buying it," he said, stretching his back.

Seeing that his bag was nearly full, she stepped over the row and hoisted the sack to her shoulders, waving him off when he protested. Liv walked quickly to the end of the garden and gingerly placed each head of cabbage in the box, waiting patiently in the back of her dad's old pick-up. Grabbing the handles of the now empty bag, she returned it to her father.

Taking a deep breath, she exhaled loudly. "I don't think I can handle being here for Christmas," she said, her voice a whisper.

Her dad simply nodded, reaching out a hand and squeezing her shoulder before he returned to his task. Tears stung the corners of Liv's eyes, making it challenging to find the center of the tightly packed leaves. She squeezed her eyes shut and quickly brushed the moisture from her cheeks.

※ 3 ※

"I know, Matt, I'm so sorry to leave you dealing with this, but I'm literally leaving for the airport right now," Liv said into her Bluetooth, tossing a few more warm sweaters into her suitcase.

"I don't know what to tell the client," Matt said, his voice tense. "It's like the entire company just fell off the face of the earth."

"We've emailed? Called? Messaged on social media?"

"All of it. No response."

"Well, I'll have to put together another floor plan with a different sofa option. But I won't be able to have that for them until tomorrow evening at the earliest. And that's *if* I find a suitable replacement with reasonable ship time," Liv deliberated out loud, biting her cheek.

"Should I tell them we'll need to reschedule that in-home consultation?"

"No, just smooth it over," Liv said, pulling her suitcase to the front door. "I'll get it done."

"You're sure?" Matt asked skeptically.

"Positive. Once I land, I'll get right on it. Sonya's good for the consult Friday, right?"

"Yep, we're all set once we have that design finalized."

"Thanks, Matt, I'll get it to you," Liv said, waving to her mother in the car waiting for her in the driveway.

"Sorry, work stuff," Liv said, her face flushed as she threw her suitcase in the trunk and settled into the passenger seat, shutting the door quickly to keep raindrops from hitting the interior.

"Hey, I get it. It's got to be hard running a business remotely," her mom said, pulling out to the street.

"Thanks for driving me."

"There are perks to living by family."

Liv nodded, then stared at the windshield wipers swishing back and forth across the glass in front of her. The street lights ahead seemed blurred and muted through the relentless droplets.

"So, Tamara gets here next week?" she asked.

Her mom nodded.

"I'm excited to see them for New Year's," she said, attempting to muster real positivity and excitement in her voice.

"It'll be good to at least get a little time all together before they leave," her mother said, her tone rife with disappointment.

"I'm sorry I can't be here for the whole visit," Liv lied.

"It's alright, honey. I know you've got a lot to worry about and take care of. I get sentimental around the holidays, but we're going to see a lot of each other this next year. It's not the end of the world."

"Thanks, Mom."

"Is it going to feel lonely being all by yourself for Christmas? Do you at least have friends you're getting together within the city?"

Liv blushed involuntarily, remembering she hadn't told her mother the truth about her trip. Not wanting to add to the deception, she attempted to be natural yet vague.

"I'm sure I'll be able to arrange something. But I've got a lot of appointments scheduled. It might actually be nice to sleep it off on Christmas day."

"Well, I hope you'll at least order a nice dinner if you don't have time to cook."

"I'll be fine, Mom," she said.

Her mother hesitated, tapping her fingers on the steering wheel. "Do you ever...I mean, do you still see Connor's parents? I know you had such a good relationship."

"No," Liv shook her head, looking down at her hands. "I haven't heard from them since he filed."

"They didn't even call to hear your side of the story?" she asked.

"No," Liv repeated softly. "I guess...whatever Connor told them was compelling enough to keep them away."

"Maybe we could send them a letter or something, with copies of everything you gave the judge—show them how he was the one who cheated on you and—"

"Mom!" Liv cut in, exasperated. "It's okay. I appreciate your concern, but I'm just trying to put it all behind me."

"It's not right—"

"I know," Liv said gently, putting an arm around her mother's shoulders as she drove.

Liv's flight was uneventful—thankfully—but upon landing in Denver, she was immediately thrust into post-aviation chaos. It seemed the entire airport was under construction, and after discovering a third re-route of her carousel in baggage claim, she threw her hands up in frustration. Her self-imposed deadline weighed heavily on her as she rushed to the new location. She needed to put that final design together. Driving to the Cottages was going to take at least an hour, and it was already two o'clock in the afternoon. So much for having any time to relax or settle in.

She finally found her suitcases circling on carousel number four. Heaving them to the floor, she rushed to ground transportation with the wheels clacking on the tile behind her. Signs for public transportation were fairly obvious, and it took her only a few minutes to navigate to the Uber pick-up point. Setting her bags next to her, she opened the app and called her car.

Six minutes away. She watched the animated vehicle with great interest, tapping her foot impatiently as it maneuvered along the curves of the digital airport roads. Hopefully there wouldn't be any traffic through the city at this time of day. But, if the internet data was sufficient on her phone—which, at least right now, it seemed to be—she could potentially hotspot her laptop and work in the back seat. This thought calmed her considerably. She took a deep breath and held it for a few seconds. With that extra hour, she could meet her goal, no problem.

She pulled a protein bar from her purse and quickly ate it before the black sedan pulled up to the curb. No three-star rider reviews for her today. Leaning over, she tossed the wrapper in the trash can, then walked to the back of the vehicle to double-check the license plate. Confirming it matched the information in her app, she slid her suitcase into the open trunk, closed it, and hopped into the backseat with her purse and her laptop bag.

· · ·

At three-thirty, the car slowed, and Liv surfaced from her technological trance. Old-timey buildings slid into view outside her window, nestled between large Ponderosa Pines and snow-covered streets. Feeling much less stressed with a decent amount of work under her belt, she put her laptop away and gazed past the glass. It seemed surreal. She wasn't a stranger to snow, but white, soft blankets draped over the branches of lush evergreens were new; even in the mid-afternoon, she could imagine how the town looked when the strings of lights between the shops were twinkling in the twilight.

Excitement built in her chest. She was about to have *two weeks* to relax and explore on her own terms. This thought transported her back to the only other mountain getaway she'd experienced...with Connor. Last November, they'd been in Tahoe to ski with his friends from college. She shuddered, remembering how he'd told her she'd gained weight and probably shouldn't wear that swimsuit in public. Or how he'd insisted she come along on ski runs she had no business attempting, then abandoned her halfway down the mountain to catch up with his buddies.

That was their marriage in a nutshell. Somehow, when they'd been dating, she'd convinced herself that he was pulling her out of her shell—helping her be brave enough to take advantage of new opportunities and learn new skills. But he'd been showering her with affection and praise back then. Going out of his way to effusively flatter her. When that ended, all of their adventures didn't seem quite so fun anymore.

About a mile past town, they pulled through the trees and under a sign that read "Holiday Cottages Farm."

"Which one's yours?" the Uber driver asked.

"Ummm, let me check," Liv muttered, scrolling through her phone and landing on the confirmation email. "Looks like it's Holly Bough Cottage," she said, "but there doesn't seem to be a map or anything..."

"No problem, we can drive around the property," her driver said.

Liv opened the Uber app to preemptively leave a tip as the car turned along the country road. A sign on the left advertised Christmas trees for sale, and there were couples and families milling about. Something about this place was already bringing a smile to Liv's face. It seemed staged—like a fictional, Christmas storybook land where these were all actors, playing a part in an immersive work of art.

"Or, your cottage could be the first one on the left," the driver chuckled, pointing out his window. "Holly Bough, right?"

"You got it. That's definitely convenient," Liv said, organizing her belongings as the car pulled to a stop.

The driver stepped out into the snow and pulled her bags from the trunk. Liv—though she'd been sure she'd chosen well by wearing her ankle boots—looked at the knee-height snowdrifts and balked. Thankfully, when she opened her car door, she saw a path had been plowed along the street and up to the cottage. Still...she may need to purchase some proper snow boots at some point. And it's not like they'd go to waste —she'd have plenty of use for them when she inevitably made her way back to New York.

"Thank you," she said, taking her luggage handles from her driver's outstretched hands.

"Do you need help up to the door?" he asked.

"No, I think I'm good."

He nodded, and she gave a small wave as he sat back in the driver's seat and drove away.

4

The interior of the cottage looked exactly as expected. It was definitely not her style, but again, in this make-believe location, it fit exquisitely. Garlands stretched along the trim of the door and front window, tiny Christmas villages adorned the mantle above the fireplace, and a cozy blanket was draped over the loveseat. Glancing in the kitchen, she noticed a plate of fresh cookies on the table.

Oh, she could definitely do this for two weeks. She sighed contentedly as she removed her boots and pulled her bags to the bedroom. A rustic, wooden bed sat in the middle of the room, and she couldn't help herself. She jumped onto it—disturbing the neatly tucked holiday quilt—and laid her head on the pillows.

After a few much-needed moments of relaxation, she pried herself from the plush mattress and opened her luggage, neatly tucking her clothes in the dresser drawers, charging her electronic devices, and placing the empty bags into the closet. There. She had completed her only actual chore for the day. Now, she could work in peace.

Removing her laptop from the dresser and its charger from the wall, she walked to the living area and plugged it in there instead. Having accomplished so much on the drive, she wasn't stressed at all about completing this proposal on time. She quickly copied and pasted a few photos, drew up some finishing details in the design blueprint, and adjusted the pricing worksheet.

In less than an hour, she pressed 'send' on her email to Matt. Done. Now that it was completed, she felt silly being so anxious about getting it sent. Not surprising, though. She'd never worked well with unknowns, and as much as she reminded herself to be optimistic and flexible, it definitely wasn't her strong suit. At least, now she could genuinely enter relaxation mode.

Liv hadn't been entirely dishonest with her mother about the amount of work that needed to be accomplished before Christmas...she'd simply left out the fact that she'd turned most of it over to the rest of her team. In years past, she'd been the point person on most accounts, and she didn't have someone as reliable and detail-oriented like Sonya to turn things over to. Now that she had more experience under her belt, Liv trusted her completely and was more than happy to turn over the reins. And Sonya—motivated to build her portfolio—was more than happy to work and earn bonuses over the holidays. It was a perfect marriage. Her only perfect marriage, so far.

Thankful she'd been paying attention as she drove through town, Liv felt confident that the grocery store was only a mile or two away from her cottage. Grabbing her black, down puffy coat from her room, she pulled her scarf and mittens from her backpack, slipped the key to the cottage in her pocket, and headed out the door.

The mountain air was crisp, and the chill felt refreshing against her cheeks. The cold air hit her lungs like a punch to the gut, and she coughed a few times before acclimating. She immediately wrapped the scarf around her neck and pulled her mittens on. Though the sun was shining, her body had clearly already forgotten how to deal with cold. All it took was a few weeks in Florida to undo years in NYC, apparently.

Liv walked briskly and took another look at the Christmas tree sales on her way past the entrance, then allowed her attention to shift to the beautiful spruce trees on either side of the road. There was no guessing where the town got its name. She walked, taking in the smell of needles and forest mulch, eventually spotting the town ahead of her.

She turned onto Pine Street, heading toward the shops. She passed a quilt shop and laundromat, and her imagination ran wild, writing a small, hopeful part for herself in this play. In a different life, could she live in a small town like this? Run a little coffee shop, go hiking on the weekends, be satisfied with a simpler life? It sounded idyllic, but she was all too aware of her propensity for restlessness. Still. For two weeks, it could be fun to pretend.

Without any timeline, she meandered along the street, popping in and out of shops that caught her interest. Unable to resist, she purchased a hot cocoa piled high with whipped cream and chocolate shavings from the little cafe on the corner. As she walked the remaining block to the grocery store, she grasped the foam cup with both hands and, with each sip, it warmed her inside and out.

A bell tinkled as she walked into Nature Pine's Market, and she easily spotted a basket in a stack next to the produce section. Realizing that shopping with a basket in one hand and a drink in the other would prove difficult, she took a moment to finish her hot chocolate and tossed the cup in the wastebasket near the front door.

Even shopping for groceries, she felt like she'd stum-bled into a real-life Pinterest page. The produce was displayed in adorable wooden crates with signs overhead written on rustic chalkboards. The variety wasn't overwhelming, but she didn't need much. She put three apples in a bag, then picked out a head of lettuce and a few other vegetables. With a couple of boxes of pasta, salad ingredients, and chicken breasts, she could survive the weekend no problem. And tortilla chips. With cheese and salsa.

Moving to the cereal aisle, she grabbed a bag of locally made granola and a box of instant oatmeal, then found her way to the refrigerated section. Setting her basket on the ground, she opened the glass door and reached in for a container of vanilla yogurt. Spinning around, she placed it in her basket and picked it up by the handles. Not looking ahead of her, she walked along the narrow aisle and jumped back in surprise as a man lumbered around the corner.

"Oh!" she gasped in surprise, grateful that she was no longer holding a hot drink. Looking up at the source of her disturbance, she held her breath. His blue eyes were hidden behind dark lashes, and his hair was tantalizingly unruly. Her breath caught in her throat, and she gripped her basket with both hands.

"Sorry," he mumbled, moving past her hastily.

Liv's heart was still pounding as she made her way to the register. It had been a while since someone had stopped her in her tracks like that. She'd been in New York far too long if a mountain man with a five o'clock shadow could leave her speechless.

"New in town?"

"Hmm?" Liv said, looking up at the checker.

"Are you new in town?" she repeated.

"No, unfortunately," she laughed. "I'm only here for a couple of weeks."

"For Christmas?" the woman asked, brushing her platinum hair out of her face before sliding the box of granola across the glass.

"Yep, I'll be here until the 27th," Liv said as the woman counted her apples.

"Here with a family?"

"No, just...by myself. I needed a little relaxation."

"Well, this is the perfect place for it," she grinned, but Liv noticed the slight look of pity in her eyes.

"Have you heard about the caroling?" the woman continued.

"No," Liv shook her head.

"It's right out here," she pointed down the street. "Six-thirty to seven-thirty in front of the entrance to the Holiday Bazaar. We have groups from all over the state that come and perform each night leading up to Christmas," she explained, scanning the last of Liv's groceries.

"I didn't see a bazaar when I pulled into town," Liv said, her eyes wide with excitement. "Are there quite a few vendors?"

"Oh, you wouldn't have seen it coming from the highway; it's another block south—right in front of City Hall. And yes, for a small town like this?" she laughed, watching as Liv scanned her credit card. "You'll find everything from pastries to handmade soap. And they take cards," she added, winking.

"Well, thanks for the tip," Liv said, grinning. "I'll definitely check it out."

"You can come say hi to me if you do. I help most nights at the cider stand from seven 'til close."

"Nice to meet you," Liv said, walking toward the door. "I'll stop by."

"Welcome to Sprucewood!" she called after her, and Liv waved as she stepped into the brisk winter air.

5

B ack at the cottage, Liv unloaded her groceries. A mile didn't seem like a long walk until she was carrying grocery bags and her arms already ached from walking through the store with a full basket. She'd stripped off her coat, scarf, and mittens upon walking through the door, but now she wished she still had them on. Was she chilled from her walk or was it abnormally cold in here? Setting her dinner on the counter—she'd passed by a sandwich shop and couldn't resist a BLT with homemade chicken noodle soup—she checked the thermostat. How had it dropped *ten* degrees since she'd left? She shifted the needle even further to the right, but when she checked the vents, they remained quiet and lifeless.

Quickly flicking on the fireplace, she rubbed her hands together. Seriously? The heat decided to quit within hours of her arrival? What did that say about the rest of her trip? She pulled out her phone and flipped open the binder that sat on the edge of the counter. The first laminated page labeled, 'Welcome!' held the information she needed. 'For emergencies, call—' she read and quickly typed the number in.

The phone rang more times than she would've liked, but eventually, a man's voice answered.

"Hello?" he said, his voice low.

"Hi, ummm, is this the correct number for the Holiday Cottages?" she asked, suddenly questioning whether she'd dialed correctly.

"Yep."

Liv waited for more explanation, but it never came. She continued awkwardly. "I'm calling because—well, I'm staying in Holly Bough Cottage. I just checked in a few hours ago, and I went to grab a few things in town, but when I came back—" she stopped to take a breath. "Are you still there?"

"I am," he said stoically.

"So, when I got back, it was freezing in here. I tried turning up the thermostat, but it won't respond. I think it might be broken."

"You said Holly Bough?" he clarified.

"Right."

"I'll be over in a minute," he said, hanging up before she could say thank you.

When he said 'a minute,' he wasn't kidding. Before she could even pull her food from the paper bag, fill a glass with water, and settle in at the kitchen table to take her first bite, a knock sounded at the door, and she rushed to open it. Twisting the handle, she pulled it toward her and sucked in a breath. It was him—the rugged guy from the grocery store.

"Can I come in?" he asked, and Liv noticed his hair was damp. It glistened in the porch light, and was most likely beginning to freeze in the cold air.

"Yes, of course. Sorry," Liv said, tripping over herself as she moved out of his way.

He slipped off his snowy boots, revealing dark blue wool

socks, and took the few steps down the hall to the narrow closet that held the heater. He opened the door and leaned in, holding a small flashlight.

"It's the pilot light," he said to himself, then reached into his pocket for a lighter. "Should be good now," he continued matter-of-factly. "But let me check the thermostat just in case."

Liv nodded as if she had suddenly taken great interest in HVAC, though her effort was utterly wasted. He wasn't even looking her direction.

Pulling a few small tools from his pocket, he used a screwdriver to open up the casing and peered inside. Then, with a small brush, he dusted the mechanism and again used his flashlight to get a better look.

"There's some corrosion here," he muttered. "I think it would be a good idea to replace it." He glanced toward the vent, still not hearing anything. "I'm guessing you don't want to spend the night sleeping in here by the fire," he joked, turning toward her and setting the casing he'd removed on the counter, along with two tiny screws.

"Not ideal," she admitted and saw a slight grin appear on his lips. Her heart leaped.

"I've got a couple of thermostats at my place," he said. "Did you have anywhere to go right now or can I come back and get it fixed for you?"

"No," Liv said, shaking her head. "I mean, I was thinking about going to the bazaar to see the caroling in about an hour, but I think it happens every night, right? I can always go tomorrow."

"You'll have plenty of time," he said, checking his watch. "Be right back."

He slipped past her, pulled on his boots, and walked out the door. Liv's shoulders relaxed—she hadn't even realized she'd been tensing them—and she took a deep breath. Her hands felt jittery, and she mentally chastised herself for being so immature. This man was simply doing his job. A beautiful, beautiful man doing a beautiful—ugh!

She ran her hands through her hair. What was happening to her? He probably had a wife and kids, for goodness sake. This thought sobered her. Of course he did. Hard-working, handy, attractive—this guy was definitely taken. Grieving the endless possibilities that had sprung up in her mind upon seeing his face at her door, she settled quickly into acceptance.

Still...it wouldn't hurt anything to look her best. She quickly ran into the bathroom to touch up her hair and put on a little makeup. After a day of traveling, she was more than slightly a mess. Not wanting to obviously change her appearance, she washed her face and pulled her hair up into a loose bun. She rubbed moisturizing cream into her skin, balm on her lips, patted concealer under her eyes, and used an all-purpose highlighter on her cheeks.

A knock again sounded on the door, startling her. She walked down the hall and opened it.

"I thought you said you had to go get a thermostat?" she asked with a hand on her hip, honestly confused at seeing that he'd returned so quickly.

"I did," he said, another smile barely playing at the corner of his mouth.

Taken. She reminded herself. One-hundred-percent taken.

He motioned to the cottage just down the road from hers. "I'm staying right there."

She looked at him quizzically. "Are you—do you work here? Or are you another renter?"

This brought on a laugh, and Liv had to feign interest in the door frame to keep herself from staring at the dimple that gloriously appeared in his left cheek.

"I work here. That cabin isn't decked out like this one,"

he said, motioning to the Christmas paraphernalia. "But the thermostat works, so I can't complain."

Liv grinned, moving to make room for him to step inside. "So you live there? Full time?" she asked, her heart skipping a beat. There's no way he could be hiding a whole family in a cottage this size.

"For now," he answered simply, again slipping off his boots and walking to the thermostat. Though dissatisfied with his abbreviated answer, Liv couldn't think of a way to ask for more information without being socially awkward.

He hesitated before reaching the wall, then turned around. "I need to go into the bedroom to hit the breaker."

Liv nodded, and he disappeared down the hall. She hoped it wasn't a mess in there. Her stomach grumbled and—not knowing how long this repair was going to take—she walked into the kitchen, finally taking a much-awaited bite of her sandwich. It was no longer hot, but it wasn't cold either. Good enough.

Standing up, she searched for a spoon and found one in the drawer next to the stovetop. She returned triumphantly to the table and opened the styrofoam cup of soup. She ate self-consciously, fully aware that he wasn't paying any attention to her, but nervous nonetheless. As she took her last bite, she looked up to see Mr. Fixit waiting patiently for her to acknowledge him.

"All finished," he said, and she nearly choked as she attempted to swallow her food without chewing.

"That was fast," she said after washing down her bite with a gulp of water.

He shrugged. "Looks like it's working, but if you have any trouble, you've got my number," he said, pointing to the binder.

Her heart flip-flopped, and she pursed her lips. "Thank you."

"No prob," he said, already putting his boots back on.

"I'm Liv, by the way. Looks like we'll be neighbors for the next two weeks."

"Two weeks? That's a longer stay than normal."

"Is it?" she asked. "I'd think plenty of people would come up here to escape for a while."

"In the summer, sure, but not around Christmas," he said, standing up straight.

Liv could feel her face darken. Of course nobody came up here alone for the holiday.

"I'm Jonah," he said softly, a look of concern briefly crossing his face.

"Nice to meet you," she said, forcing a smile. "Thanks for your help. I'll think very grateful thoughts as I crawl into bed tonight."

Jonah chuckled, then gave a small wave as he stepped out onto the porch, closing the door behind him.

6

Very grateful thoughts as I crawl into bed? Seriously? Liv's already wind-rubbed cheeks blushed under her scarf as she walked toward town. It was much colder than it had been this afternoon and, though she'd expected as much and worn every stitch of warm clothing she'd brought, it didn't seem to be helping much. Within ten minutes, she was shivering, and she hadn't even made it past the grocery store.

Looking across the street, she noticed what looked like a warm flannel jacket hanging in the window of a shop called All Spruced Up. The name made her chuckle, and she made a beeline for the door, hoping beyond all hopes she'd be able to find something to layer under her coat. Otherwise—no matter how beautiful the singing was—this wasn't going to be a particularly pleasant evening.

"You look cold," a young woman said as she entered. Her hair was dyed bright red and pulled up into a loose ponytail.

"I didn't bring enough warm clothes," Liv laughed, rubbing her hands together, gratefully soaking in the warm inside air.

"Where're you from?"

"That's a complicated question," Liv said, "but most recently, Florida."

"That's slightly warmer than here," the woman laughed, and Liv noticed the slight sparkle of a tiny nose stud as her face lifted. "So, what are you looking for?"

"Something warm to layer under my coat," Liv said, glancing around the shop.

"I've got fleeces over here," the woman said, moving from behind the counter and directing Liv to the back corner.

"Oh, these look perfect," Liv said, choosing a grey size small from the hanger.

"Want to try it on?"

"Are you kidding? I'm going to wear it out of the store," Liv laughed, stripping her jacket off and pulling on the soft sweater.

"Well, at least let me take the tags off," the woman said, hustling back to the register and grabbing a pair of scissors. Liv lifted her hair to the side and allowed the woman to snip the price-tag from the fleece.

"Ooh," she said. "Do you happen to have any actual snow boots?"

"That's the *only* kind we have," the woman laughed. "What size are you?"

"Eight," she said, watching the woman walk to the other side of the store, rifle through her stock, and return with three different boxes.

"I don't have a lot, but there are a few options," she said, opening the lids to show her. Liv's eyes landed on a pair of black Sorel boots lined with faux fur. They were low profile and waterproof. She pulled one out of the box and—pulling her own boot off—tried it on. It fit like a glove.

"I'll take them," she said gratefully.

"Perfect," the woman said, setting the other two boxes to

the side. "Will you be wearing these, too?" she asked, lifting the scissors.

"Absolutely," Liv laughed, putting her boots into the box and taking the other new boot from the woman's outstretched hand.

"What's the damage," Liv asked.

"Well, it's fifteen percent off, so that makes it $84.57 with tax."

"Not bad," Liv said, pulling her credit card out. The woman swiped it, then handed her a receipt to sign. "Thank you so much; these are going to be complete life-savers."

The woman smiled, putting her shoebox into a paper sack. "Are you heading to the bazaar?"

"I am, first time."

"You'll love it. Welcome to Colorado," she said warmly as Liv walked back into the cold, bag in hand.

Feeling much more comfortable, Liv walked another block, already hearing magical chords bouncing in the air as she approached the entrance of the bazaar. Lights twinkled around her as she found a spot on the sidewalk to watch the choir. Her heart swelled as she took in the group of youth— bright smiles on their faces, eyes fixed on their director, and voices swelling to the chorus of "We Wish You a Merry Christmas."

Beyond the singers, people bustled between the booths set up on the lawn of City Hall. The scene took her back to a Christmas trip she'd taken as a child. Come to think of it, she didn't actually know where her family had gone that year, but she distinctly remembered walking through a market like this, lights and all. Thinking of her parents sent a pang of guilt through her, and she folded her arms across her chest, hugging tightly.

After enjoying another song, the cold again began to seep in, and Liv knew she needed to keep moving. She dropped a few dollars into the bucket on a stand next to the choir director and walked under the archway. Immediately, her senses were overwhelmed with the smell of cinnamon, fried bread, and chocolate. This might be a dangerous place, considering her current emotional state.

She perused the shops, picking up a small jar of hand lotion and lip balm from a local apothecary. Buying a bag of mini donuts, she thought about sitting at one of the open tables in the middle of the square but couldn't bring herself to sit alone. That, and the fact that her day of travel and work-stress was finally catching up to her. She yawned, turning back the way she came, when she saw someone waving at her. Liv smiled, walking over to the cider booth to greet the checker from the grocery store.

"You made it," the woman said, smiling broadly.

"I did, great recommendation."

"Really gets you in the Christmas spirit, doesn't it?"

Liv nodded but felt an emptiness to the motion. "You said you volunteer here?"

"Anyone in town takes a shift. Well, mostly everyone. Some of us are more willing than others."

Liv grinned. "Well, thank you for putting that time in. Normally I'd get a cup, but I already bought these," she said, motioning to the bag of doughnuts she gripped in her left hand. "This is really magical."

A couple approached the booth, and Liv backed away to make space for them. She waved at her new friend and headed back toward the arches.

Thankfully, Liv passed many others strolling along the road back to the Holiday Cottages. She was a tad nervous about walking alone after dark, though this seemed to be one of the least intimidating places to do so. Once the trees thinned, she could see her porch light in the distance and couldn't wait to cozy up for a movie in her warm living area with that soft blanket she'd been eyeing all day.

She reveled in the stillness around here, the fresh mountain air, and the moonlit sky above her as she walked. There was something exceptionally peaceful about being outside in the cold and dark when the earth itself seemed to be sleeping. Street lamps bathed the path in pale yellow light as she approached the cottages, and she watched people afar off, milling around, still looking for that elusive, perfect Christmas tree.

"You're back early," a voice sounded on her left, and Liv jumped.

"You scared me," she said, turning to find Jonah sitting on his porch. "How are you sitting out here in only a long-sleeve t-shirt?"

Jonah shrugged. "It's not that cold yet."

"I beg to differ," Liv said, shivering. This time, not from the frigid temperature. "Well, have a good night. Don't freeze out here. I'm no good at cleaning up dead bodies," she said, continuing toward her cottage.

Jonah didn't respond, and Liv forced herself not to turn around as she turned the key in the lock and stepped inside.

7

Liv opened her eyes, confused at first by her location. Had she fallen asleep on the couch? Looking down, she found herself dressed in her outfit from the night before. She must have been more tired than she thought. At least she'd turned off the television. Sitting up, she stretched her arms over her head. Her neck was only slightly stiff, considering her awkward sleeping position.

After visiting the bathroom, she walked into the kitchen for breakfast. Her eyes widened when she saw it was already ten in the morning. Panic took hold for a second before she remembered there were no deadlines to meet today. Still, taking a detour, she searched for her phone in her purse by the door. Twenty-seven messages. Good grief. Forgetting all about food, she slumped again to the couch and began to scroll.

Thankfully, even though most items were from Matt, they were easily approachable. Sighing in relief, she returned to the kitchen and pulled a bowl from the cupboard. Pouring in two packets of oatmeal, she added water and put the dish in the microwave. Today was going to be fantastic, she decided.

A little work to accomplish, but then she had committed to at least six chapters of a book and another chick flick. Definitely another chick-flick.

She ate her oatmeal—the cinnamon-sugar almost like dessert—and then moved on to her tasks for the day. Setting up her laptop at the table, she took a moment to catch up on her social media accounts. Immediately, she noticed a message from her friend Sara in New York. Clicking on it, her heart stopped.

>*Liv, did you see Connor is engaged!?*

She re-read the message three times. Engaged? They'd only been officially divorced for a month. Her heart was racing as she searched for his Facebook profile. She'd blocked it a long time ago, which is why she wasn't privy to his latest romantic conquests.

The page loaded, and the image slammed into her. There was Connor. An arrogant smile on his face—as usual—with his arms wrapped around a gorgeous—tiny—woman with jet-black hair. That woman couldn't be more opposite from her in looks. Literally her exact opposite. Liv's thoughts began to spiral—all of her insecurities bubbling freshly to the surface. Tears sprung to her eyes, out of frustration, anger, or sadness; she couldn't tell.

Not able to help herself, she clicked on the woman's profile, scrolling through her recent posts. Of course she was an actress. And vegan. Sighing in disgust, she slammed the top of her laptop closed and wiped the moisture from her cheeks. Never-mind about the work. That would have to wait until later, because right now? She needed movie therapy. ASAP.

. . .

Two romantic comedies later, Liv was sprawled on the couch with red-rimmed eyes and a runny nose. She pulled a tissue from the end table and blew. Though she didn't necessarily feel any happier about the whole Connor situation, at least she'd been able to cry.

"I hate him," she whispered to herself, but even as the words left her lips, she knew it wasn't true. She hated who she'd become with him. And she hated that he somehow still had a hold on her.

She forced herself to shower, dry her hair, and put on clean clothes—even if they were yoga pants and a t-shirt. It counted. Though she technically had food to eat, she had absolutely zero motivation. Pulling on her new boots and old coat, she walked out the door and headed into town.

Lost in her own mind, she almost didn't see Jonah walking back toward his cottage from the Christmas tree display. He waved, and she wished she had a scarf to hide her puffy face.

"Were you 'very grateful' last night?" he asked, close enough now for his voice to carry without shouting.

Liv stared at him in confusion before it clicked. "Oh," she said, her face blushing. "Yes, I was toasty warm; thank you."

When Jonah didn't say anything else, she scrambled. "So what exactly do you do around here? Do you—I mean, are you an owner?"

He laughed. "No, definitely not."

This time Liv waited patiently. She was not going to be the one to keep this conversation going every single time they talked. If he wanted to stand in awkward silence, so be it.

After looking at the trees a moment, he finally spoke. "I used to be a middle school teacher."

"Oh," she said, taken aback. He didn't seem like the teacher type. "Used to? You're not old enough to retire. And that doesn't explain why you have stockpiles of thermostats in this cottage."

The dimple appeared again on his cheek, and Liv looked away.

"I haven't taught for a few years. I've been between jobs. This is a temporary handyman position. Pays better than teaching."

"Just for the season?"

"Their regular guy got hurt on the job. I was the next best option," he shrugged.

Liv mustered her courage. "Are you married? Have a family? Live close by?" She added that last one in, hoping to seem casual in her questioning.

Jonah ticked the questions off his fingers. "No, complicated, and yes."

Liv's interest piqued. "Complicated?"

"Complicated," he repeated.

Liv nodded. "I understand complicated."

"My house is just over that hill," he said, pointing south of town.

"It's empty right now?"

He nodded. "They insisted I live on property. And I don't mind saving on the water and electric bills."

"I certainly benefited from the convenience of having you close," Liv said without thinking. "For the pilot light. And thermostat," she added hastily.

Jonah shoved his hands in his pockets, an amused twinkle in his eye.

"Well, I'm heading to get some lunch," Liv said, turning to go.

"Stop at Phil's," he called after her. "Best sandwiches in town."

She turned and nodded, then continued on her way, feeling better than she had all morning.

8

Liv pulled a fresh cookie from the plate on the table —her reward for finally staying on task that after-noon. She had no idea how this chocolate chip perfection kept appearing out of nowhere, but tonight she couldn't have been more grateful. She had just taken a chewy bite when a knock sounded on the door. Her heart leapt, knowing she had only one or two real acquaintances in town, and they had no idea where she was staying. Did they? But why would *he* be here at this time of night? She swung the door open, and her face instantly fell.

"Good evening, ma'am," a man said overly enthusiastically, his face unfamiliar. "I'm walking around, letting every guest know about our horse-drawn sleigh rides around the farm. We didn't want you to miss it."

He handed her a flyer and gave a chipper wave as he hopped down the steps. Was he wearing elf shoes? Closing the door, Liv looked at the small slip of paper in her hands. 'Magical sleigh-rides under a starry sky,' it read. Liv crumpled it up and threw it decidedly in the trash. Going solo on a romantic sleigh-ride was exactly what she *didn't* need after a day like today. Just one more potent reminder of her failed relationship.

Another knock sounded on the door, and she whipped around, opening it with mild annoyance.

"Hey," Jonah greeted her, flustered by her abrupt appearance and the cloudy expression on her face.

"Oh, I'm sorry, I thought you were—"

"Flyer guy?" Jonah cut in, pointing over his shoulder.

"Yeah, flyer guy," she sighed.

Jonah looked at a small package in his hands. "He's...excited about his job."

Liv laughed.

"You looked a little upset earlier this afternoon," he continued slowly. "I was roasting chilies over at the main pavilion and...I thought you might like some."

"Oh, wow," Liv said, taking the foil-wrapped offering. "That was really thoughtful, thank you."

He nodded, pausing slightly before retreating down the steps. Liv began to close the door when Jonah's voice caught her attention.

"I have to go to that sleigh-ride thing tonight," he said, scuffing his feet in the snow. "I know I don't know you that well, but I figured...we're both here alone and doing stuff like that is—" he sighed, taking a breath. "It's kind of terrible alone."

Liv paused, processing his words. "Are you asking me to come with you?" she asked tentatively.

"If you don't want—"

"No, that sounds like fun," she said. "When?"

"Now," he said, looking somewhat sheepish.

With shaking hands, she answered, "Oh, okay—ummm let me go grab some warmer clothes." She closed the door and leaned against it for a moment, catching her breath to calm her racing heart. What was this? Worry immediately cropped up within her. She was vulnerable—especially after seeing Connor's post this morning—and he was cute. More than cute. And single, if she understood his answers correctly earlier. And...complicated. Did she really need more of *that* in her life? But this was just a sleigh ride, not a marriage proposal. It's an hour of my life.

Nervous and a little excited to do something she knew was likely risky and wonderfully irresponsible, she ran to her room, put on her fleece and a pair of socks, then ran back to the door to finish bundling up.

"Okay," she said, finally opening the door. "Ready."

With hands still in his coat pockets, he nodded toward the tree farm, and Liv followed, her heart still pounding. She took a deep breath.

"You *have* to go tonight?" Liv asked.

Jonah nodded. "Those sleighs are about a hundred years old. It's always fifty-fifty whether something's going to break or come loose."

"How often do they do this?"

"Twice a day. I only go a couple times a week."

"So you sit on the sleigh and ride along every Saturday?"

Jonah nodded. "That's my night of choice, usually. I don't have much going on on the weekends. Again, terrible, I know."

"Well, glad to help out."

They walked a few moments in silence, and Liv noticed the plumes of steam billowing up from their noses with each breath. How cold was it tonight? Either her new gear was doing its job beautifully or she was beginning to acclimate. She didn't feel nearly as uncomfortable as she had the night before.

"So where are you from, Liv," Jonah asked, still looking straight ahead.

"Originally from Pensacola, but then I moved to New

York about seven years ago," she sighed. "Now I'm back in Florida."

"Same place?"

"Yep. About fifteen minutes from the house I grew up in."

"You don't sound too happy about that," he teased.

"That's because I'm not," she said, wondering why she was being so candid with a perfect stranger. "I'm twenty-seven and moving back home."

Jonah nodded. "I'm sorry."

Liv looked up at him, then quickly refocused on the path ahead. Nobody had responded like that before when she'd expressed disappointment in her current life trajectory. They always had some tidbit of wisdom to bestow, like 'I'm sure you'll figure it out soon' or 'life doesn't always go how we planned.' She'd gotten so used to it that Jonah's simple expression of empathy felt shockingly new and refreshing.

"I'm twenty-nine, by the way," he said.

"Wow. You're an old man," Liv joked.

"Sometimes I feel like it."

Liv could sense a heaviness to that statement. Like he'd lived two lifetimes before this moment. She mentally laughed at her internal dialogue. Always so dramatic. He probably just had a bad back.

Not knowing how to respond, she was quiet as they approached the meeting area for the sleigh rides. Couples, families, and—notably—zero single people were lined up against the fence waiting for the go-ahead to load up. Two gorgeous Clydesdales were harnessed to the sleigh, bundled in blankets and jingle bells, plumes of hot breath rising from their nostrils.

"Jonah," a man dressed in long coattails and a top hat called to them. "Took you long enough, buddy."

"I brought a friend," Jonah said, nodding to Liv.

"Works for me. Want the backseat?"

Jonah nodded, ignoring his waggling eyebrows, and the man motioned for them to get on the sleigh ahead of the other riders. Liv reached the stepladder first and stretched above her head to grip the handrails. She easily hoisted herself up and walked down the center row to the back of the sleigh, taking a seat as instructed. Jonah sat next to her, and almost immediately, the line of people began to filter up the steps and into the rows ahead of them.

"So. Do you normally feel like a chaperone back here?" Liv asked.

"More like a creepy voyeur."

Liv grinned. "Where are your tools to fix this thing when it falls apart? You know, to make it look legit."

"There's a compartment on the side of the sleigh that holds spare parts and tools."

"Smart."

They politely listened as the man they'd met earlier gave an announcement about sleigh safety. Two staff members dressed in red velvet coats walked down the rows handing out large flannel blankets to anyone who wanted one. Liv signaled for her own, and Jonah chuckled beside her.

"What?" Liv scoffed. "I'm getting it for you. You don't even have gloves on. Are you going to sit with your hands in your pockets the entire ride?"

"I usually do," he said.

"Well, tonight is going to be much more comfortable for you, then. You're welcome."

A few moments later, the sleigh lurched forward, and Liv gripped her seat. After the initial forward momentum, the horses settled into an even pace, and Liv pulled the blanket up around her arms and shoulders. Around them, couples cuddled, pointing up at the night sky, and children begged for snacks from their parents who kept reminding them they had just eaten dinner, and they needed to remain seated.

"This isn't the worst place to be a creepy voyeur," Liv whispered, and Jonah laughed.

"It's entertaining, that's for sure."

"Why don't you just bring your phone along or something? If you have to do it every week, you may as well get some work or socializing done while you ride," Liv asked.

He turned to her with a quizzical look.

"What?" she asked.

"What kind of work do you do on your phone?" he asked skeptically.

Right. His work wasn't something he could complete over google docs.

"I'm an interior designer. I own my own business; it's called Liv In Designs. Original, I know, but I liked the play on words—do you get it? 'Liv' instead of Live?" Jonah stared at her blankly. "Anyway," she continued, "I communicate a lot with my team every day, and I often make design tweaks or order pieces online. My phone is kind of a big deal."

Jonah nodded. "Hence, New York."

"I mean, you can be an interior designer anywhere. I did want to try to make it there, but I was more..." she began to explain, then trailed off when she realized where that sentence was heading.

Jonah waited patiently.

"I was more moving there to support my husband's dream," she finished, and Jonah shifted uncomfortably in his seat.

"Ex-husband," she clarified. "We separated last year and the divorce was finalized last month."

Jonah seemed to relax, but he didn't respond immediately. Liv clutched the blanket and listened to the muted clomping of the horse's hooves in the snow. Had she said too much too soon?

"I was married before," he said, pulling her attention away

from potential conversational missteps. "We were divorced six years ago."

"I'm sorry," Liv said, copying his response from earlier.

"It was my fault," he admitted, and Liv turned to him. When she saw the hurt written on his face, she wanted to say all the cliches like 'it takes two to tango' or 'love is a two-way street,' but she couldn't bring herself to do it. Those words had become hollow to her, and considering how often he *didn't* speak, Jonah didn't seem like a man who'd appreciate superficiality.

"Well," she sighed. "My divorce was his fault, so I guess we don't have much in common where that's concerned."

Jonah laughed out loud, and the couple in front of them turned around in annoyance.

"Sorry," she said quietly. "That was insensitive."

Jonah coughed, attempting to gather himself. "No," he said finally. "That was perfect."

Liv blushed. "It's honestly nice to know I'm not the only damaged single person out there."

"Definitely not," Jonah said.

The sleigh reached the end of its route and turned to head back to the farm on a parallel trail. This path took them past snowdrifts nearly as tall as the horses, and Liv was entranced by the evergreens, barely poking their heads out of their deep winter blankets.

"I've only got two weeks here," Liv said, "so I think—if we're going to be friends—we should probably just get everything out in the open sooner rather than later."

Jonah raised an eyebrow, giving her a sidelong glance.

"I'll go first," she offered. "My ex's name is Connor. We met through a mutual friend in college. He was tall, charismatic and charming—always the life of the party. He wore these round, almost antique glasses that I thought were intriguing at the time." Liv paused. "I'm not sure what that has to do with anything."

"I'm glad I don't wear glasses."

"Other glasses are fine, just not...*those* glasses."

"Noted."

"Anyway, we dated for six months before he proposed, and then we were married a year later. Part of that time we lived apart—him in New York and me still in Florida finishing up my degree. Not once did I doubt that he was anything other than the perfect guy I'd envisioned him to be." Liv paused, taking a deep breath. "Spoiler alert. He was cheating on me. The entire time. During our engagement, the entirety of our five-and-a-half year marriage. I'm just grateful we didn't have kids."

Jonah's jaw clenched as he stared ahead.

"So, there you have it," Liv concluded. "As you can imagine, I'm horribly insecure because of all that and—to top it off—I lied to my own, lovely parents about having a heavy workload over the holidays so that I could avoid Christmas dinner with my family."

Jonah raised his eyebrows, whether out of amusement or disgust, Liv couldn't tell. She decided to pretend it was appreciation for her honesty.

"Okay. Your turn," Liv sighed.

"I didn't necessarily agree to this," he hedged.

"True. You don't have to participate if you don't want to. Thanks for letting me get that off my chest, though. If I admit it to you, I don't have to admit it to them, right?"

"Is that how it works?" Jonah teased. He leaned back on the bench and pulled on his side of the blanket, tucking his hands under the edge. Liv grinned.

"I was married for three years to my high-school sweetheart. We both stayed local for school and we didn't get back together until I was doing my student teaching."

"What did you teach?" Liv asked.

"I didn't interrupt you," Jonah shot back good-humoredly.

"You're right, sorry. Proceed."

"I taught middle school science," he said pointedly, "but two years after I started at the school here in town, I—" he paused, clearing his throat. The light she'd seen in his eyes a moment ago seemed to fade. "It wasn't a good fit," he said finally.

Liv's brow furrowed. Was it the low teacher salary? The fact that it was middle school? She wanted more details, but the expression on his face led her to shift direction.

"So you work here now? You said it's seasonal. Do you move around to other locations?"

"No," he shook his head. "This is the first time I've done work like this. I'm a woodworker, so I make furniture in the shop attached to my house."

Liv's eyes widened. "That's incredible."

"I didn't say it was good," he chuckled. "But it pays the bills."

"Then it's probably good," she teased, elbowing him lightly.

The sleigh pulled back into the glow of the street lamps surrounding the tree farm, and Liv sighed reluctantly. This had been an unexpectedly good night, and she didn't want the ride to end just yet.

"Hey, no repairs," she said, sitting upright.

"Free ride tonight," he nodded. "Thanks for coming with me. It was good to talk to someone."

"It was good to talk," Liv agreed, blushing as he caught her eye. "And now that I got out and did something, I won't feel the least bit guilty about watching another movie before bed."

"*Another* movie? How many have you watched?"

"Sharing time is over," she teased, pulling the blanket

dramatically off their laps and folding it into a precise square. Waiting their turn, they slowly followed the line of people off the sleigh, and Liv handed the blanket to one of the staff members waiting near the horses.

"Are you walking back?" Liv asked.

"No, I need to help put the sleigh and horses away for the night. Do you feel comfortable heading back on your own?"

"Sure," Liv lied. "No problem."

As Jonah turned to the man in the top hat, Liv pulled her coat around her and walked quickly in the direction of her cottage. That was fun. And weird. She didn't know this guy at all, yet she'd basically word-vomited all of her darkest life moments of late. Maybe that had freaked him out? Is that why he didn't say much about himself? Liv recounted the conversation, analyzing her comments and questions. What was she thinking, being so open with someone she'd just met?

With self-doubt spinning uncontrollably inside her, she turned up the path to her door. A good 'ol movie would fix this. It always did.

9

Two cinematic productions and a plate of green chili nachos ended up being the perfect remedy for her racing mind. After crying through the first show, she needed to laugh through another, just to even it out. And yet again, Liv found herself waking on the couch with blurred makeup and stiff clothes around ten the next morning. This was her life now, apparently.

She pulled her phone from its charger and rolled over onto the pillow to check her email. Deleting the spam, she found a few urgent work items and mentally began to plan her morning. When she'd reached the end of the new items in her inbox, she swiped over to Facebook. Not able to help herself, she typed in Connor's name to see if there were any updates on his page. She was torturing herself, and she knew it, but it was too tempting.

Clicking on his profile, she was taken to a limited page with the message 'This profile is private.' Had he removed her as a friend? She didn't know why this was surprising, considering, but still. It felt like the last nail in the coffin of their marriage. Now she couldn't even masochistically spy on his new life? *What kind of world was this!?*

She laid her head back in frustration, rested her phone on her chest, and stared at the ceiling. She needed to get over this—*to get over him*—but it just wasn't happening. And the worst part? Over the past few years, most of her actual friendships had gone down the tube, as well. In trying to make him happy—and then throwing herself into her business when she couldn't—she hadn't put effort into maintaining other relationships. Now it didn't matter whether she was physically with people in New York or tucked away in a remote cottage. She was always very much alone in the world because she hadn't been inviting anyone else in.

Maybe that's why she'd spilled her guts to Jonah in the sleigh. She needed someone to know her again. Someone— anyone—to really see her and ideally conclude she was valuable in some way, shape, or form. Because right now, she didn't believe it. And yes, she knew that it was very much *not* feminist to admit to needing another human to validate you. Especially a man. But right now it felt overwhelmingly like the world was telling her she *wasn't* wanted or needed. Or even worse? The world didn't notice she was there at all.

Before she spiraled too far, she lifted her phone and clicked on Messenger, scrolling to the message from her friend Sara. She hadn't ever responded to her tip about Connor's engagement, and now that she couldn't troll his page, she needed to talk about it. And Sara happened to be online.

Hey, sorry for the late reply. I checked it out. I hate how pretty she is 😔

>I knew you would 😂 But I couldn't NOT tell you

Agreed. I'm glad I heard it from you before stumbling across it. But, just found out he unfriended me, so maybe I wouldn't have seen it anyway!

>*Ugh. But kind of a good thing, right? He's not worth your time.*

I know...

>*He treated you like crap, Liv.*

I know

>*I feel like maybe you don't know* 😭

I do. I think it'll just take time.

>*Hey! At least now we could get together—are you interested in a work out buddy?*

I would LOVE a workout buddy...but I moved back to FL for the time being. Be close to family and all that.

>*What? I just saw Matt a few days ago and he didn't mention anything. When did this happen?*

Recently. I didn't tell many people—I don't want clients to think I won't be available.

>*Will you be available?*

After the holidays I'm going to schedule a few days a month to be in the city. I'm hoping that will work. Cheaper than living there full-time. I needed a change.

>*I hear that. Nice that you can work from anywhere.*

Liv felt a pang of guilt, knowing Sara didn't have that kind of flexibility. She'd been attempting to work up the ladder of her advertising firm for years without much progress. She was still putting in long hours and making plenty of sacrifices of her own without much to show for it.

Random q. How would one theoretically attempt to get over a failed marriage?

>*Lots of chocolate.* 🍫🍫

Another q. It would never be a good idea to spend time with an incredibly handsome guy in a location you were staying in temporarily...right? Asking for a friend...

>*Ok, scratch the chocolate. Your 'friend' should definitely spend as much time as possible with said handsome stranger and enjoy every second of it. What has she got to lose!? If it goes south, who cares?*

What if he's a nice guy?

>Even better. If you're up front about being there short-term, he'll understand it's not like you're looking for something serious. And you one hundred percent need to get out there again. Meet new people. See something different.

Thanks, Sara. I'm sorry I haven't been a good friend the past few years.

> ♥ I get it. Let me know when you're back in the city, k?

Will do.

There. She still had friends, right? At least one friend. That was something. And who cares if she made a fool out of herself last night? Jonah was the one who'd invited her along in the first place.

She swung her feet to the floor and walked to the kitchen. Dumping some yogurt in a bowl and smothering it in granola, she made her way to the door. Pulling on her boots, hat, and scarf, she grabbed the blanket from the couch and stepped onto the porch. It was colder than she would've liked, but the sun was shining, and she had a perfect view of Jonah's cottage. It was ridiculous to think he'd be home at this hour, but if he were...maybe she'd get lucky and catch his eye.

She sucked in a breath as she sat on the chilled bench, then quickly tucked the blanket underneath her to buffer the cold. Once she was comfortable, she took in the scenery around her. It really was beautiful here. Snow slowly melted from the branches of the evergreens, dripping until being shaken loose and adding to the drifts on the ground beneath the trees. Birds sang and chittered to one another, swooping between the trees, seeming to glory in the warm rays of sunshine.

Hearing the sound of a door opening, she looked to the right and spotted Jonah kicking his boots on the edge of the porch before opening his door and stepping inside. That was anticlimactic. Sitting in the cold just for that? She laughed internally at the ridiculousness of this whole venture. And yet she still didn't want to leave the icy bench.

Then—just as she'd taken another bite—the door opened again, and Jonah stepped back onto the porch. He looked her direction, and she waved. Was that a smile? She couldn't tell from here, but he immediately headed toward her.

"Morning," he said, breaking from the path and walking through the drift to approach her side of the porch.

"Hey," she grinned. "Already working?"

He nodded. "Just came home to grab a tool."

"No rest for the weary."

He smiled, his dimple making its first appearance for the day. "You didn't get enough of the cold last night?"

"I wanted to take in the scenery this morning," she said.

"What do you have planned for the day?"

She held up her hand, creating a zero with her fingers. "Vacation, remember?" she teased.

Jonah nodded.

"What about you?"

"I'm working."

Right. Stupid question. "I meant after work," she hedged.

"I was going to go catch the hockey game in town."

"You don't have TV in that fancy place?" she asked, gesturing toward his cottage.

"I do, but watching the game at Phil's is tradition."

"Huh," Liv nodded. "What time?"

"Five-thirty."

"Well, if it's tradition...maybe I'll stop by. Get a taste for the local scene."

Jonah grinned. "Don't wear red."

Liv looked down at her cranberry sweater. "Couldn't this be an Avalanche color?"

"Pushing it," he grinned. Jonah trudged off and—as soon as he was out of sight—Liv hustled inside for some warmth. And a change of color.

10

Liv walked through the door of the sports bar to a rush of warm air. The sounds of jovial conversation and dishes clattering enveloped her as she searched the room. It wasn't busy enough for Jonah to be lost in the crowd, and she definitely didn't see him. Just as she was wondering whether she should take a seat at the bar and wait or head back out the door, a voice caught her attention.

"Hey!" a female voice called, loud enough that Liv sensed it was directed at her.

She turned toward the dining room in surprise, then smiled as she recognized the woman walking toward her. Her red hair landed just above her shoulders in loose, wavy curls—not pulled back like it had been the other night—but the small nose ring gave Liv confidence she had the right person. "You work at that shop. You sold me these boots," Liv laughed, pointing to her feet.

"Good memory. Glad they're working out," the woman smiled. "Did we exchange names? I can't remember. I'm Paige."

"Liv," she said with a smile.

"From Florida, right?"

Liv nodded.

"Are you here to watch the game?"

"Kind of?" Liv laughed. "Someone—a friend—invited me to meet him here to watch the game, but I don't think he's here—"

"Someone you're traveling with?" Paige cut in.

"No, uh—" she hesitated. "This guy I met up with at the Cottages."

Paige raised an eyebrow. "Oh, yeah?"

"Nothing like that," Liv assured her. "He basically had pity on me and gave me an opportunity to get away from work and...sappy Christmas movies."

Paige laughed out loud. "Well, who is this mysterious benefactor?"

"His name's Jonah—" Liv started, but quickly stopped when she noticed the look on Paige's face. "Is that—?" she began again, but was interrupted by a blast of cold air from the door opening behind her.

"Speak of the devil," Paige muttered, looking past Liv's shoulder.

"Good evening," Jonah said, and Liv turned to greet him.

"Didn't realize you were bringing extras tonight," Paige said, a hint of annoyance in her tone.

"Didn't think you'd mind," he said evenly.

"Me?" Paige said, her eyes flashing. "Nope. The more the merrier."

"I don't have to—" Liv said, but Paige cut her off.

"No, c'mon over. We've got a table, and we haven't even ordered apps yet," she said apologetically, putting an arm around Liv's shoulder and pulling her toward their group. "He just never tells us if or when he's coming, so it threw me for a loop."

Sitting down at the table, she watched Paige for any more

clues that would explain the odd interaction she'd just witnessed, but was disappointed. Jonah chatted with the bartender for a few moments, then joined the group—pulling up a chair at the end of the booth, already staring at the TV on his right.

Liv was preemptively doing a google search on her phone for details about the game; she'd watched hockey last season in New York, but hadn't paid any attention during the months since. Mainly because she didn't have anyone around to suggest watching sports anymore. At least she knew who the Flames were.

"Liv, anything for you?" Paige asked after yelling an appetizer order across the restaurant.

"Just a Coke," she said, "but I can go put that in myself."

"Another Coke, Bobby!" Paige shouted to the bartender. Taking a seat, she pointed at the other four people in the circular booth. "This is Neil, Ryan, Zack, and Krista."

"Hey, I'm Liv."

"Did I hear Paige say you're from Florida?" Zack asked. He looked exactly like a few of her skateboarder friends back home. He had jet-black hair and grey textured gauges the size of skittles in his ears.

"Yep, I'm taking a break for a couple weeks. Needed some R&R."

"Maybe that's what I should tell Monarch. I need a break," Neil said, feigning exhaustion, and Krista elbowed him. Neil was cute, and by the way he carried himself, he was well aware of that fact.

"What's Monarch?" Liv asked.

"Ski resort," Jonah said, rolling his eyes at his friend's antics. "How many days before you start the holiday rush?"

"Oh, it's already here," Neil said, brushing his sandy-blond hair out of his eyes. "Mountain's packed."

"And when Monarch's packed, you know people are desperate," Zach laughed.

"Whatever," Neil said, "Just because it's not commercialized by Vail? It's charming. What skiing *should* be."

"I don't think you can call it 'skiing' when you sit on those rickety lifts for half the day," Zach shot back, throwing a wadded up piece of his napkin in Neil's direction.

"Boys, boys, you're both pretty," Krista laughed, pretending to break up the confrontation. As she stretched her arms out, Liv could see she was athletic. Her long-sleeved t-shirt did nothing to hide the definition in her arms, and she looked as if she was ready to spring into action at any moment.

Before any new arguments could break out, the bartender arrived with their drinks and two plates of loaded nachos.

"Now the game can start," Ryan said, reaching a hand toward a particularly cheesy pile of chips. He seemed to be the quietest of the bunch, and his outward appearance matched his personality.

Liv found her Coke on the table and pulled it toward her, then took a sip.

"Hey," Jonah said quietly on her right.

She grinned. "Hey."

"Glad you came?"

"A little early to answer that, don't you think?"

Jonah laughed, following her gaze to the boisterous group around them.

"C'mon," he said. "I want you to meet Bobby."

Scooting out of the booth, Liv followed him across the restaurant to the bar. An older man—mid-fifties—was cleaning glasses with a white cloth.

"Bobby," Jonah said, and the man looked toward them. "This is Liv. She's visiting Sprucewood for a few weeks."

"Welcome," Bobby said, extending a hand, and Liv shook it. "Just seeing the sights?"

"Just needing a change of pace," Liv said.

"This is a good place for that."

"So it seems," she grinned.

"You're up at the Cottages?" he asked. "I assume that's where you ran into this guy."

"She was being really picky and wanted her heater to work," Jonah teased, then turned to Liv. "Bobby's been like an older brother to me the last ten years."

"Thank you for not saying 'father,'" Bobby grinned.

"You definitely look too young to be his father," Liv said.

"I think I like her," Bobby laughed. "You ever need anything while you're here, let me know. Unless it's heater related, then you're stuck with him."

"Thanks," Liv laughed. "Everyone is so welcoming here."

"There are pros and cons to living in a small town," Bobby said, wiping the counter with a wet cloth, "but 'welcoming' is kind of our specialty. It'd be hard to survive through mud season without our winter and summer visitors."

Liv gave him a questioning look.

"Spring and fall," Jonah explained. "Everything turns to mud with runoff or new snowfall that melts with warmer weather."

"Ah," Liv said. "Well I'm happy to help."

"Looks like the rest of your food's here," Bobby said, nodding behind them.

"So nice to meet you," Liv said, following Jonah back to their group.

The game ended at nearly eleven o'clock. Colorado won, which meant the locals were thrilled—especially because the

Avalanche had won with a last-minute goal deep in third period. Liv had been easily swept up in the excitement and conviviality around her. For the most part, she'd felt comfortable throughout the evening, despite the fact that she'd only known these people for a few hours. It felt oddly exhilarating to reinvent herself for an evening. Nobody here—well, besides Jonah—knew anything about her past. They didn't ask questions, just laughed with her and made her feel included. She needed more of that in her life.

As everyone settled up their bill, Neil leaned over to her. "We're going to the hot springs after the mountain closes tomorrow. Want to come?"

"Dude," Jonah muttered. "Seriously?"

"What?" Neil asked innocently. "Liv said she wanted to experience all that Sprucewood has to offer. She's not going to read about *those* on Google, so she needs someone to take her."

"And you're offering to be her guide? Out of the kindness of your heart?" Jonah said, raising an eyebrow.

"Of course," Neil said, holding up two fingers. "Scout's honor."

"Uh-huh," Jonah scoffed.

"Hot springs do sound amazing," Liv said.

"Which cottage are you at? We could swing by and pick you up," Neil offered.

"Who's 'we'?" Jonah asked skeptically.

"All of us here, dude," Neil said, gesturing to their friends. "Except I'm not sure—Hey!" he yelled across the table. "Krista, are you in for tomorrow?"

"I think so, but I might have to come later. I'm not positive I'll be off in time."

"I can grab you," Zack offered, stacking plates and picking up napkins. "Just text me when you're ready."

"Thanks, man," Krista said, giving him a fist-bump.

"There you have it," Neil said, turning back to Jonah. "But, you're not planning to come, right? I know you don't—"

"I'll come," Jonah said, cutting him off. "I can bring Liv up. That way, you don't have to drive all the way back to town. We'll meet you there."

Neil's jaw clenched. "Well...that's helpful. Thanks," he said, nodding. "Glad that worked out."

Jonah grunted, and Liv thanked him for the invite, then pulled her coat on and wrapped the scarf around her neck.

"I'll walk with you," Jonah said to her under his breath. "See you tomorrow, Bobby," he shouted to the bar.

"Later!" Bobby said, not looking up as he worked to fill drink orders for a few late-night customers.

Jonah walked past the hostess stand and held the door open for Liv. She gasped as the chilly air hit her face.

"I thought I was doing better with the cold here until right this second," she laughed, wrapping her arms around herself.

"If you think this feels cold, just wait till you're in a bathing suit."

"Whatever. It can't be that bad. I can run from the springs to the changing room, right?"

Jonah laughed. "There isn't a changing room at these hot springs."

"What do you mean?" Liv asked with growing concern.

"Haven't you been to a natural spring before?"

"Like...how natural?" she laughed.

"Like 'hike in for a half-mile, strip down, climb over rocks in the pitch black, then hike back to your car' kind of natural," Jonah said, shoving his hands in his pockets.

Liv looked to his face for any hint of a joke. "You're serious."

"One-hundred percent. It's pretty amazing, and you won't

find any tourists there. It's kind of a town rule that nobody takes out-of-towners."

"But...I'm an out-of-towner. So why'd he invite me?" Liv asked as they walked up the drive to the farm.

Jonah gave her a side-long glance.

"What?" she asked, her boots crunching on the hardened snow.

"You honestly have no idea?" Jonah said, grinning.

Liv shook her head. "He's trying to be nice? He thinks it's pathetic that I'm alone here over Christmas?"

Jonah chuckled. "Oh, he's trying to be *really* nice, but it's not because he thinks you're pathetic." When Liv didn't respond, he continued. "He was flirting with you all night. And the fact that you knew players' names? That only made it worse."

"He was not; he's just friendly."

Jonah shrugged. "It's true. You've known him for a few hours, and I've known him my entire adult life. You're probably right."

Liv laughed, "I'm not buying it! I'm...not that kind of girl, Jonah."

"What do you mean?"

"You know, the girl who shows up somewhere and magically attracts a guy she's never met. That isn't me. I'm the girl someone goes to high school with and then doesn't remember I was in any of their classes."

"That's pretty specific. Has that happened to you?" Jonah asked, grinning.

"More than once."

"But you were married," he said, nudging her arm. "That means you caught someone's attention."

She gave a sarcastic laugh. "Okay, yes, you're right. Let me give a caveat to my prior statement: 'unless you are a narcissistic sociopath looking to prey on someone who isn't smart enough to see the red flags, I won't make an impression on you.'"

Jonah stopped and put his hand on her shoulder, turning her toward him on the path. He looked at her intently.

"I've known my share of selfish people, and the people they hurt aren't stupid," he said thoughtfully. "The people they hurt are usually so kind, they can't imagine someone wouldn't be."

Liv held her breath, then let it out slowly. "It's a nice thought, but even my parents thought I was stupid. They called everything before I married the guy, and they thought I was—"

"They were wrong," Jonah said, letting his arm drop to his side, leaving a breath of heat on her shoulder where it had been resting.

"Thanks," she said, her voice a whisper.

Turning, they walked a few moments in silence, and Liv lifted her eyes to take in the clear, starry sky. Exhaustion from the long night began to set in just as their Cottages came into view.

"Thanks for the great night," Liv said.

"Glad you had fun."

"Hey," Liv called as Jonah turned to walk to his door. "Why—" she cleared her throat. "Umm, why did Paige seem upset that I was there tonight?"

Jonah's shoulders lifted as he pushed his hands deeper into his pockets. His unruly hair fell across his forehead as his brow furrowed.

"It's complicated," he said slowly.

"Mmhmm," Liv nodded, waiting for more explanation. When it didn't come, she smiled graciously and said, "See you tomorrow," then continued on the path to her cottage.

11

L iv woke the next morning with a stiff neck and a dull headache. She hadn't slept well, despite her physical fatigue. It wasn't like her to wake up during the night, but she had. Multiple times. And each disruption had been connected to a nightmare of some sort.

She couldn't remember every disturbing detail, but one scene in particular played over and over again in her mind as she got out of bed to use the bathroom. She was at the restaurant from last night—sitting in the booth with all the same people—when Connor had walked through the door, waving his signature swagger around like a flag on the Fourth of July. Everyone turned to observe him, which is what he wanted, of course, and what had attracted Liv to him in the first place. Because, when she was with him, all eyes were on her, too. She didn't feel like *that girl* in the background anymore; she felt...like something. Important.

The ironic thing was that Connor didn't ever intend to share that spotlight. He just sucked the life from her in an attempt to make himself brighter. Having her there made him seem even more untouchable to other women, which, as it turned out, only made them try harder. The ironic thing about that? They didn't have to work that hard to get his attention. Yet Liv did. Every day.

In her dream, he barely paid her any notice. He flirted with Paige and Krista, then made fun of her outfit in a way that could have been interpreted by onlookers as good-humored, but she knew better. It was a purposeful strike. Jonah was sitting next to her, and he laughed right along with everyone else at Connor's jokes and digs.

Her heart pounded as she washed her hands. It was a dream. She knew it was a dream, but the emotions felt so real and...devastating. Why couldn't she be free of him? Was this a not-so-subtle reminder that he'd always be there? That she couldn't even reinvent herself for a night without him swooping in to put her back in her place? Liv was exhausted and upset, and it wasn't even ten o'clock in the morning.

She heard her phone buzzing in the other room and hustled to answer it.

"Hey, Mom," she said.

"I didn't wake you, did I?" she asked, concern in her voice.

"No, you're good," Liv sighed, hopping back on the bed and pulling the covers over her.

"How is everything going?"

"Great, I'm getting lots of work done."

"Do you think there's any chance you'll be back for Christmas?"

Liv rolled her eyes. "No, Mom, I told you I wouldn't—"

"I know, I know," she sighed, "I was only hoping that maybe it would work out."

"I'm sorry," she said quietly, and she meant it. She wasn't sorry to be missing everything, but she was incredibly sorry that she wasn't capable of handling it.

"It's okay, honey," her mom said, rallying herself. "We had a great day at the market this weekend."

"That's awesome," Liv said. "And shouldn't Tamara and the kids be there in a couple of days? Didn't you say the 21st?"

"Yes, they'll be here Thursday. I think I've got almost all the breakables put up on high shelves."

Liv laughed. "Good job."

Her mom paused before speaking, then asked tentatively, "You're sure you're not too lonely?"

"I'm sure, Mom. I'm busy and...figuring some things out."

"Good for you," she said. "I know this hasn't been an easy year."

"That's an understatement."

"You know we're here for you, right?"

"Of course," Liv said, shifting her position.

"Find something fun to do for Christmas Eve, promise me?" her mom said, almost scolding her.

Liv laughed. "I promise."

After cleaning herself up for the day—but not washing her hair since it was only going to be pulled up in a bun for the hot springs—she made herself a mug of herbal tea, turned on the fire, and cozied up on the couch to charge through her emails.

Before she went to bed the night before, she'd received word that the orders she'd scrambled to complete the other day had all come through. Crisis averted. Despite the uneasiness from her dream, she at least felt some relief as she opened her files this morning. If she could do regular old work for the remainder of her trip, she'd be thrilled.

Jonah arrived a few minutes before six holding two take-out containers.

"Have you already eaten?" he asked.

"No, I made some pasta for lunch around two-o'clock, so I figured I could wait until after to grab dinner."

"Well, Bobby sent me with two Cobb salads if you're interested."

"No way! That was incredibly nice of him," Liv said, moving to the side and waving Jonah in. "We won't be late if we eat first, will we?"

"No, we've got plenty of time," Jonah said, setting the containers on the table and reaching into the silverware drawer for a couple of forks. "Plus, then we can end with a cookie. If you're sharing," he grinned, looking at the plate on the counter.

Liv noticed his dimple and the way his lashes seemed to brush his cheeks when he smiled. "Yeah, I'm absolutely sharing," she said, walking to the table and sitting down. "I didn't realize these would be showing up every single day! It's amazing, but I'm pretty sure my jeans aren't going to fit by the end of this trip."

"Who cares. It's Christmas," Jonah said.

"That's easy for you to say. You're a guy."

Jonah waved her off. "Girls put too much pressure on themselves."

His comment made Liv think of her dream. Connor mocking how she looked, and Jonah laughing. She cleared her throat. "You don't get these at your place?"

He chuckled, "Nope. Cookies are only for paying customers."

"And you're not going to tell me how they show up on my table or my front step?"

Jonah mimed his lips being zipped shut.

"Well," Liv continued. "Plan on taking a few from me each day. I don't need four cookies every night!"

He shrugged, taking a seat across from her and opening his styrofoam clamshell.

"This is fantastic," Liv said, already a few bites in. "I didn't really look at the menu last night, but I wouldn't normally think to order a salad at a sports bar."

"He does a good job. You'll have to try the stuffed avocado sometime."

"Mmm," Liv said, taking another bite. "How was work today?" she asked after swallowing.

"Good, pretty typical. A couple of clogged drains, a door handle that needed to be replaced, ice removal around the main walkways—"

"What do you do if there's nothing that needs to be done on any given day?" she asked.

Jonah chewed for a moment before answering. "Go into town. Help friends. Sometimes I go work on my own place if I have a bigger chunk of time."

"Do you have any family close—" she stopped short, noticing his immediate discomfort. "Right. Complicated."

They ate for a few moments in silence, giving Liv plenty of time to ruminate on the reasons for Jonah's silence. It didn't necessarily bother her that he kept avoiding specific topics, but now that they were spending more time together, it would be nice to have a little bit of info. She trusted that he was a good person, but it did feel a bit odd that he knew more about her life than she knew about his. What was he so afraid of?

"Are you ready to swim?" Jonah asked, scooping the last of the lettuce from his container and standing to throw it in the trash.

"I've got my suit on under this and a towel in that bag," she said, pointing to the door. "Do I need anything else?"

"You might want a water bottle."

"Good idea," she said, walking to the bedroom and grabbing her travel bottle from the dresser. Coming back into the kitchen, she quickly filled it and added it to her backpack. "Ready."

"After you," Jonah said, reaching out and pulling the door open, a cookie in his right hand.

The drive was uneventful but pleasant. Jonah asked about her growing up, and she regaled him with stories of beach bonfires, swim meets, and work on the family farm. She told him about the time her dad took up Gar fishing, and she spent nearly half the year's Saturdays with him in the swamp.

Jonah told her about his ski racing days—he insisted he wasn't ever good enough to advance past local competitions, but judging by his build and how hard he was trying to downplay it, she assumed he was probably pretty impressive.

He talked about how much he loved teaching, and again she wondered why he wasn't going back to that when he so clearly loved it. Something didn't add up. First, he was single and that seemed wrong on so many levels. Second, he had a degree, experience, and plenty of practical skills. As much as he insisted that he liked the slow life in the mountains, she couldn't understand why he would settle for a life of loneliness. Well, that wasn't exactly true. She *could* understand it...which only made her more positive that he was hiding something.

They parked along the side of the road in what seemed like the middle of nowhere. Liv tucked her pants into her boots, grabbed her backpack, and zipped her coat closed before stepping out into the night.

"This is where you tell me you've brought me into the woods to murder me..." she said, stepping carefully along the tall drift.

"The path's over here," he said, not acknowledging her comment and shining a flashlight into the trees.

"I lived a good life," she muttered, following his light into the thicket. As soon as she stepped into the trees, her feet landed on a path where the snow was packed, making it easier to walk.

"See?" Jonah laughed. "Other people have been here. I'm not crazy."

"You guys were right, though," she said. "There's no way anyone could find this from Google maps. It didn't look like there was an opening from the road."

"Pretty great, right?"

"So what would happen to me if I went and published this all over the internet?" she asked, taking a few more steps and then turning when she didn't hear Jonah behind her. She shrieked as a snowball hit her directly in the chest.

"Rude!" she laughed, brushing herself off and reaching out for a handful of snow.

"Your hands are going to freeze," he teased, turning off the flashlight to hopefully hide his location. Luckily, there was still enough twilight on the horizon to allow her to see his silhouette. She formed the ball and tossed it at him, but he dodged it easily.

"You had the element of surprise," she complained.

He walked directly in front of her. "Here," he said. "Free shot."

"No way. I'm going to get you when you're least expecting it," she warned, and Jonah laughed.

He walked toward her and moved close, lifting his hands toward her head. Her heart fluttered as his hands gently covered her ears.

"Your ears are going to freeze," he said softly, his face inches from hers. "I have an extra hat in my bag if you want."

"Sure," she said, her voice shaky. Jonah stepped back and swung his bag off his shoulder, then reached in for the hat. After a moment of searching, he found it and handed a soft, knit beanie to her. In the dim light, she couldn't make out the color, but she put it on her head, realizing it was big enough to cover her bun and still reach over her ears. She tucked in a few loose hairs around her face.

"Better?" Jonah asked.

"Mmhmm," Liv said. "Thanks."

"This way," he said, leading her on through the trees. She took a deep breath to calm her nerves, then quickly followed after him.

"Y ou made it!" Paige greeted them as they walked through the trees into a small clearing. There was a lantern sitting in the snow, and she could easily see the path at this point.

"How long have you been here?" Jonah asked as they walked forward. "I thought we might beat you, but then I saw your car on the road."

"Only about fifteen minutes," Neil said. "Perfect timing."

"This is incredible," Liv said, taking it all in. In front of her, steam billowed from a series of pools, making it nearly impossible to view the surface of the water.

"Are Krista and Zack here yet? I can't see the other end of the pool," Jonah asked.

"No, you beat them. I'm assuming they'll be here in a half-hour or so," Neil said, still not visible to Liv through the clouds.

Drifts of snow swept gracefully atop the rocks, the ledges, and faces of some boulders bare from the geothermal heat. Tree branches sparkled around the clearing and Liv walked to examine the pine needles closest to her. They were completely covered in a thin layer of ice, glistening as she moved them in the lantern light. The effect was pure magic.

"I love watching people discover this place for the first time," Paige said, and Liv grinned as she walked back to the edge of the pool. The steam was so thick; she could still barely see anything until a breath of air shifted the fog away from their side of the clearing. It was then that she saw Jonah standing only a few feet in front of her, lifting his shirt over his head and setting his clothes next to his backpack on top of a tarp that someone stretched out over the crystallized snow.

Not wanting to stare, she hastily walked to the tarp and set her bag next to his, pretending to search for something so she didn't have to change right there beside him. She stood and watched as he carefully navigated the rocks and lowered himself into the hot water.

"I'm not going to slip, right?" she said, pretending she'd been carefully inspecting his mode of entry and not the muscles on his upper back and shoulders.

"I'll help you," Neil assured her. As he came into view through the steam, she couldn't help but notice his athletic build. The fact that everyone in this group seemed to be stepping out of a fitness magazine made her instantly self-conscious. It made sense; they were all into the outdoors and active, but still. It was going to be quickly apparent when she stripped down to her bathing suit that she was...not. Her figure was curvier, and that was one thing she typically liked about her body. But next to all of this? She felt soft and weak. Physically inferior.

Shaking these thoughts off as best she could, she slipped her feet from her boots and stepped onto the tarp, sucking in a breath as the cold plastic hit her skin. Moving fast, she unzipped her coat and slipped off the rest of her clothing, hoping the fog would add some sort of cover.

"Okay, follow where Jonah went," Neil instructed, still close to the edge, "and then reach for my hand."

She followed his instructions, walking quickly across the snow and lowering herself down the rock. She found his outstretched hand and allowed him to hold some of her weight as she stepped into the water.

"Oh, wow," she said.

"Feels amazing, right?" Neil laughed.

"What temperature is this?" she asked, her teeth clenched, and her breathing quickened to manage the discomfort of stabbing pins and needles in her feet.

"It's about a hundred and four," Paige said on her left.

"The bottom of the spring is surprisingly comfortable on my feet," Liv said, finding a spot next to Neil where she could lean against the rocks along the edge.

"I know. I've been to a few pools near Breck where the bottoms were quite sharp. This one's way better," Ryan said.

"Are there a lot of them around here? I had no idea," Liv said, her body fully relaxing into the heat.

"Not a ton. There are a couple more commercial ones, like Glenwood Springs," Neil said.

"I've heard of that one," Liv replied. "Never been there, though."

"You're not missing much," he said. "Unless you like crowds. However, the town itself is definitely worth the visit. Really cool hikes and rafting there."

Liv took a deep breath, closing her eyes. "This is heaven," she said.

"Worth the walk?" Jonah asked.

"Definitely," she said. "Thanks so much for inviting me, you guys. And you don't have to worry. Jonah already answered my question of what would happen if I posted this on Instagram."

"Scared her, did you?" Paige said, moving closer to Jonah.

Her hair was pulled up into a short ponytail, and she wore a knit warmer around her ears. Somehow, she was able to pull off cute and edgy at the same time. Liv's stomach turned as Paige slid an arm around Jonah's back, nestling close to him.

"See? He won't bite," she said.

Liv forced a smile, but quickly looked away before she could see Jonah's reaction.

"Is this the first time you've been up here this year?" Neil asked, looking toward Paige and Jonah.

"It is," Jonah said curtly.

"Isn't this where you met—"

"That's enough, Neil," Jonah warned, his voice low. Neil held his hands up in defense. "Sorry, sensitive subject."

Liv watched the interaction with concern. Neil was purposefully goading him, but why? Weren't they supposed to be friends?

Turning to Liv, Neil continued, "Well, I'm not worried about you outing us on Facebook," he teased, splashing water on the rock behind him to melt the snow, then hoisting himself up to take a seat. "But, you *do* have to pass an initiation test."

Liv turned toward him, raising an eyebrow. "What does this 'initiation test' entail?"

"Observe," Neil said flirtatiously. Grateful for an excuse not to watch Paige and Jonah, she leaned on the rock with her eyes on Neil as he carefully walked across the snow, holding onto a tree branch for stability.

"Okay, so once you're up here, you have to fall backward —" he said, and she gasped as he completely disappeared in a drift of pristine, white snow. He immediately popped back out—covered in white sparkling crystals from head to toe— and moved as fast as he could back to the pool.

He jumped in with gusto and purposefully landed next to Liv, pressing his freezing cold back against her arm and shoulder. She screamed in shock and desperately pushed him away from her. He laughed and sunk past his shoulders to warm up.

"You're turn," he teased, and Liv shook her head.

"I'd kill myself attempting that! Do you know how unco-ordinated I am?"

"Nope," Neil shook his head. "And that will *not* get you out of this. You'll just have to be careful and go slow."

She stared at him, grinning. "You're seriously going to make me do this?"

"One hundred percent," he laughed.

Liv braved a glance in Jonah's direction to find him sitting alone. He wasn't looking at them, and it seemed purposeful.

"It's not that bad, Liv, I promise," Ryan chimed in. "You've got to do it at least once."

"Has to do what at least once?" a voice called from the trees.

"Krista!" Paige shouted with excitement. "Just in time. Liv is about to snow dip."

"Wait for us to get in so we can see!" Zack said, and Liv could barely observe their outlines moving in the direction of the tarp.

Great. All she needed was a bigger audience. Despite the heat, her body began to shiver. She didn't want to be the loser who wasn't gutsy enough to freeze in the snowbank, but *she was also terrified of freezing in the snowbank*. No part of her found that desirable. Though, she also knew from past expe-rience that doing something out of her comfort zone did bring a certain sense of pride and accomplishment. And who really cared if she looked like an idiot? Jonah obviously had something going on with Paige that he wasn't telling her about, and it wasn't likely that she'd ever see them again after she went home. What did she have to lose? If there was ever a time to let loose and look like an idiot, it was now.

"Fine," she said firmly. "I'm game. But if I slip and die, it's on your head," she teased, flicking water towards Neil's face. He lit up at her announcement, yelling to Krista and Zack to hurry up. A few moments later, they stepped into the pool and Liv turned to lift herself onto the rock Neil had been on a few moments ago.

With shaking arms, she pressed her hands against the cold, rough stone and sucked in a breath as her knees hit the icy surface. She followed Neil's steps up the slope and—without allowing herself to hesitate—fell backward into the snow. She heard whoops and hollers as she frantically jumped up out of the drift. She shivered from head to toe—her skin burning from the cold—and jumped back into the pool, careful to land directly in Neil's lap. She laughed giddily at the intensity of the hot water against her freezing skin. Neil pulled her to him, pretending to love the sudden cold and she squirmed to escape his grasp.

"There, you happy?" Liv said, moving back to her spot. "I'm officially initiated."

"That you are," Neil laughed. "Impressive work."

Liv breathed a sigh of relief as the warmth permeated her being, but then glanced over and caught Jonah's face. He wasn't smiling, and his somber expression made Liv's stomach drop. He was upset; she could see that, but why? Shouldn't he be happy that she was having a good time? He'd been all over Paige a moment ago, so he couldn't possibly be upset that she'd returned Neil's flirting. Maybe Neil's reference to his ex was still stinging.

Meeting her eyes, Jonah reached into the snowdrift next to him. Forming a ball, he tossed it over between Paige and Krista. The girls shrieked and immediately began forming snowballs of their own. Liv watched Jonah doubling his efforts to pelt the two women with snow, suddenly seeming to be thoroughly enjoying himself. A weight seemed to settle on

Liv's chest. He hadn't said two words to her since they'd arrived.

"Hey," a voice sounded softly in her ear. She started and turned to find Neil next to her. "I know you came with Jonah, but can I take you home? I don't have the luxury of living at the Cottages," he said, motioning across the pool, "so I don't have an obvious way to get to know you better. And I'd like to."

Liv's heart started beating quickly, surprised and flattered by Neil's proposal. In the background, she could hear Jonah laughing and splashing around as Paige presumably succeeded in blasting him with snow.

"Sure," she said, clenching her jaw. "That would be great."

Neil smiled, pleased with himself. "Whenever you're ready to get out of here..." he said, sliding back to the rock he'd been resting on.

When the snowball fight finally died down, Liv accepted a San Pellegrino from Zack, grateful for something other than tap water to drink.

"I think I need to get out," she said, feeling a little light-headed.

Neil jumped on that comment immediately. "I'll take you home," he said nonchalantly, obviously not wanting to admit to Jonah that he'd set this up beforehand.

"I'm good to leave now—" Jonah said, but Neil cut him off.

"You haven't been here in ages, dude. Enjoy. I've got this. I have to get up early tomorrow, so I need to head out anyway."

Jonah stared at him for a moment but eventually nodded. "Are you okay with that, Liv?"

"Sure," she shrugged, walking to the other side. "And I think I'm going to enjoy the cool air on the walk back."

"It's great until the last five minutes," Krista laughed. "Then you basically have to run to your car."

Liv laughed. "Oh, Jonah, are you okay with me taking your hat home? I can get it to you—"

"No problem," he said dismissively. "I can get it another time."

Irrational anger bubbled up within her. Why was he acting like this? They'd had a fantastic talk on the way here and then...nothing. Less than nothing. Then—on top of her frustration—she heaped on a serving of embarrassment over the fact that she even cared. Why would she care!? She'd known this guy all of four days, if that?

"Thanks," she said, her voice harder than she'd meant it to be.

Liv climbed out of the water onto the rocks, tiptoed over the snow to the tarp, and quickly pulled her towel from her bag. She dried her arms and legs, then wrapped it around her torso and pulled her coat on over it. Still dripping, she pulled on her socks and boots.

"See you guys later," she said, slinging her backpack over her shoulder and following Neil who was already waiting beside her. Her boots crunched over the icy snow as they entered the cover of trees.

"So what do you do when you're working at the ski hill?" she asked, following Neil's flashlight.

"Mostly work the lifts, go after the occasional lost skier. Today we had a four-year-old girl get on the lift without her parents. That was fun."

"Do you get time to ski?"

"Oh yeah, I can go pretty much anytime I'm off. Free food at the lodge, too. It's not a 'career-plan' per se, but it's an excellent filler for a couple of years while I figure out what I want to do."

"What *do* you want to do?" Liv asked, the winter air beginning to sting the skin on her exposed legs.

"I'm planning to open my own business. I just haven't decided what direction I want to go."

"That's cool. What kind of business?"

"No, that's what I meant," Neil laughed. "I'm not sure yet."

"Oh!" Liv laughed, "Sorry, I thought you meant—"

"I know what you thought I meant," Neil teased. "You assumed I'd have thought this through and have a plan, that I only need a few design and marketing ideas, and then I can move on it."

"Is that so crazy?" Liv teased. "I mean, we are almost in our thirties."

"Maybe you are!" Neil said, gently pushing her to the side. Liv laughed, catching her balance.

"How old are you?" she asked skeptically.

"Twenty-four. Why? How old are you?"

"Well, I'm not saying now," she grinned, and Neil turned the flashlight in her direction. "No, stop! You'll see my wrinkles!" she joked, blocking her face with her hands.

Suddenly, the flashlight turned off and Liv was in total darkness.

"Neil? Did it die? Where—"

She gasped as Neil grabbed her around the waist and pulled her close.

"I don't see any wrinkles," he whispered, then crushed his lips to hers. Liv's eyes widened with shock, and she pushed at Neil's shoulders, attempting to pull away. His kiss became more insistent and—when his hand began to move under her coat and up her bare back—so did her defensive maneuvers. She shoved him. Hard.

"What was that for?" Neil spluttered.

Liv still couldn't see anything, but she could tell he was a few feet from her now.

"I could ask you the same thing," she gasped, wiping her mouth. "I tried to pull away—"

"Don't give me that," Neil chided. "You were flirting with me all night, and now suddenly you aren't interested?"

"Neil. Just because I'm friendly doesn't mean I'm hoping for you to kiss me the second time we've ever spent any time together. Seriously?"

"Okay, well, most girls on vacation are looking to hook up with some local guy, so—"

"You do this *often?*" Liv said, disgust in her voice.

"No, I didn't mean—"

"I think I've heard enough, thanks," Liv said harshly, finally able to see a few feet in front of her face in the moonlight.

"Liv, I—"

"Just get away from me, Neil!" she shouted, backing up against a tree.

"You're going to freeze out here," he said, his voice low. "At least let me take you home."

Liv shook her head. "I'll figure something out."

Neil threw his hands up in the air. "Fine. Good luck," he spat, turning on his flashlight and jogging down the path toward the road without a backward glance.

13

"Liv?" Jonah called through the trees. "Liv, are you there?"

"I'm here," she answered, walking along the path back to the hot springs. She was shivering now, all the heat from the pool long since drained from her body.

"Are you okay?" he asked, jogging around the corner, nearly running straight into her.

"I'm cold," she admitted, "but fine. How did you know I was here?"

Jonah put his arm around her shoulders and rubbed her sleeve to create heat as they walked quickly back along the path she'd just backtracked.

"I got out of the pool to change about ten minutes after you left. I had just started walking when I got a text from Neil."

"What'd it say?" she asked hesitantly.

"That you changed your mind and needed a ride," he said, dropping his arm, but still walking close to her. Liv nodded, but didn't respond.

"No comment?" Jonah asked.

"It's complicated," she said and tried to keep a straight face, but couldn't help herself. The adrenaline, fear of freezing in the woods all night, her allusion to Jonah's maddeningly vague answers, and the overall stress of the last twenty minutes made her inexplicably giddy. She started to laugh, and Jonah looked toward her questioningly.

"It's actually very *not* complicated," she said between giggles. "Neil tried to grope me, and I said no."

"He *what?*" Jonah asked, his body stiffening next to her.

"That made it sound worse than it was," she explained hastily, sobering with his intensity. "We were walking back and joking around with each other, then he turned off his light and kissed me. I tried to push him away, but—" she exhaled loudly. "He wasn't easy to persuade."

Jonah walked in silence.

"I'm sure he's a nice guy, but it seems he's grown accustomed to single women and...what they want when they're alone on vacation," she finished.

"Don't make excuses for him," Jonah said, his voice low.

"I'm not. It was a jerk move. But he's also young. And probably stupid."

"Not that young. And that's another excuse."

"I'm worried I overreacted," she whispered. "I yelled at him."

"A dude you barely met jumps you when you're half-naked in the woods and you're worried you hurt his feelings? No. You should've kicked him extremely hard in the—"

"Jonah, I'm fine. Really," she said, pulling her arms tighter around herself.

They finally stepped out of the woods and quickly found Jonah's truck parked next to the road. He opened her door for her and she hopped in, placing her backpack on her lap and clutching it to her chest for warmth.

That had been her first kiss since Connor. She'd hoped

her first romantic experience after him would've been...different. And actually wanted. Was she somehow giving off a 'please take advantage of me' vibe? Was there something about her that screamed 'I'm desperate and vulnerable'? Her teeth chattered as she stewed in the passenger seat.

Jonah turned the key in the ignition.

"I'll get the heat going as soon as the engine's warm," he promised, pulling away from the shoulder and flipping a u-turn to head back into town. They drove in silence, and Liv replayed the whole night in her head, attempting to figure out where she went wrong. She didn't find her answer, but as the reel of Paige in a bikini pulling herself close to Jonah started again in her brain for the fourth time, she did recognize something.

"What is the deal with you and Paige?" she blurted out, her jaw clenched from the cold.

Jonah sighed. "There's no deal."

"She was mad when I showed up with you the other night, and she was flirting non-stop with you at the hot spring. And you seemed to be flirting right back," Liv argued.

"You were flirting 'right back' with Neil. Did that mean anything?" Jonah needled.

Liv's nostrils flared. "No," she lied. It didn't mean anything where Neil was concerned, but it *was* a direct reaction to Paige and Jonah.

"Right," he said.

"So, all of that meant nothing?" Liv asked.

"Paige...was interested in me a while ago. I didn't return the sentiment."

"I don't think she stopped being interested," Liv said under her breath.

Jonah turned on the heater, and Liv desperately held her hands next to the vents.

"Why does it matter?" he asked, staring straight ahead at the road.

"What do you mean?" Liv asked, stalling.

"Why do you care if Paige is interested?"

"I—I don't know," she stammered. "It just seemed weird, that's all. Like maybe you would've mentioned it to me. Or at least made it clear that—" she stopped short. She didn't know where she was going with this.

"I don't typically discuss relationships with people I barely know," Jonah said, and Liv pursed her lips.

She looked out the window as they approached town, her eyes filling with tears. This was not at all how she envisioned tonight going. But what *had* she expected? The first guy she meets in town was nice to her, and all of a sudden she'd anticipated—what exactly? Whatever 'it' was, he clearly was not envisioning the same thing.

As they pulled into the lane to the Cottages, Liv hastily wiped hot tears from her cheek. The feeling had returned to her legs and feet, and she pushed her door open before Jonah had the chance to fully stop.

She pulled his hat from her head, accidentally taking her hair elastic with it. Her long blond hair cascaded around her shoulders as she searched for the band, finding it pressed between her neck and coat collar. Sweeping her hair to one side, she set the hat on the seat in front of her.

"Thanks for the ride," she said brusquely, turning and walking up the path to Holly Bough Cottage.

14

Liv woke to notifications on her phone. Dread immediately settled in her stomach, knowing that there was likely only one reason for the constant dinging. It was December 19th, and the last few days before Christmas meant crisis calls.

Taking a deep breath, she rolled over in bed and plucked her phone from the nightstand, removing it from the power cord. To her surprise, there was only one message from Matt. The rest were from Sara.

>*Hey. How is operation 'handsome guy in remote location' going? For your friend, I mean...I wanted to let you know...I ran into Connor and his new fiancee last night. She's really, really ditsy. Just thought you'd enjoy that bit of information. He's exactly the same as always.*

Liv wanted to *not* feel the selfish pleasure that filled her heart at reading this. She really, really wanted to be the bigger person. But she just wasn't. It made her disturbingly happy to hear that—though she was beautiful—Connor's new girl-friend didn't have a step on her in the brains department. And it was incredibly validating to hear that Sara saw his dominating arrogance for what it was. She was better off without him. She was.

Where did you see them? That does make me happy. I know. I'm slightly pathetic for caring. Operation handsome guy is a bust. He's still handsome. I blew it.

She swiped over to Matt's message after pressing send.

>*Christmas crisis calls are here!* 😄 *But don't worry. We've got it handled.*

You guys are fantastic, but seriously feel free to send some things my way. I'm not going to have much to do over the next few days. You'll be saving me from too many chick flicks.

>*You sure??*

Yep. Do it.

>*I love you. Check your email.*

Liv laughed and swiped back to her conversation with Sara.

. . .

> *Just at a random Christmas party. I talked with them for a bit. He asked about you.*

Liv's heart jumped, and then disgust quickly followed.

What did you tell him?

>*That I hadn't talked with you in a while, but it seemed like you were doing great.*

Perfect answer. Thanks.

>*Liv, he's such a tool. I know he talks a big game, but he doesn't have everyone fooled.*

Thanks. I think it's just going to take time.

>*We miss you!*

Liv took a deep breath. Maybe it was naive to expect a quick fix for all this. It's true. Her life hadn't gone as planned. She'd made mistakes. But she'd learned so much about herself and it wasn't the worst thing to have to start fresh. Better now than ten years from now. She still had plenty of time left to make something of herself and to find the right person. Hardly any of her friends had settled down at this point, so why was she being so hard on herself?

She reached over to the plate of cookies she'd conveniently stashed on the nightstand, grabbed one, and took a large bite. Suddenly, a thought snapped into being in her brain and she sat up straight.

She was resisting. Propping herself up on precarious half-truths to avoid the grief she knew was coming. All of the yoga she'd practiced in the city came back to her. Gratitude. Being present. She wasn't feeling *any* of that. Right now she was somehow stuck in the past *and* the future at the same time— bouncing back and forth between dashed hopes and earlier trauma. Completely unwilling to accept that her present was different than she'd imagined it. She finished the cookie and brushed the crumbs off her hands over the floor.

Well, that was going to change today. She stood up and walked to the bathroom, then leaned over the sink and splashed water on her face. Today she was going to start her practice. Life practice. She was completely capable—not only of running a business, but of adulting in general. She couldn't say that for many people she knew, even those in so-called stable relationships. That was something she could build on.

Walking to the couch, she sat down and opened Evernote on her phone. 'Gratitude' she wrote as the heading, then began to list everything she could think of. Family. Friends. Growing business. Design skills. Positive supplier relationships. Loyal clients. Good fashion sense. Healthy body. The list went on, and when she had nearly fifty entries, she looked at it in awe. She'd been missing all of this for nearly a year, and why? Because some guy said she wasn't good enough? Because he decided that he'd never be satisfied?

She laid down on the floor and stretched her arms out above her. This moment was a much-needed revelation, but she wasn't naive enough to believe she'd never feel lonely or frustrated again. Tackling this all at once was unrealistic, but she knew how to tackle big projects, didn't she? She'd never attempted to treat her personal life like she did an account at work, but maybe this was long past due.

First step? Identify the goal and make a plan. Next? Tackle the first step in that plan. Then number two, then number three, and so on. In her experience, projects simply couldn't become overwhelming when approached this way, but...she paused. The second requirement at work was that she never took big projects on alone. That was going to be a problem in this instance. Is that why she'd been avoiding so hard? Because it all seemed to land on her shoulders and hers alone? But who could she reasonably ask to assist her with this, and what would she even request that they do?

Even as she thought it, she knew the answer. Reaching her hand up to the sofa, she scooped up her phone and dialed the person she'd been avoiding the most.

"Hey, Liv! We were just talking about you!" Tamara said cheerily.

"You were?"

"The kids were asking if they'd get to see you this trip."

Liv could hear her nieces and nephews running around, chattering, and laughing in the background. "I hope you told them yes," she said.

"I did, and they're all super excited," Tamara answered, then shouted directions to her husband.

"Hey, Tam, do you have a minute to talk privately?"

"Ummm, sure, just a sec. I'm going to go outside."

Liv waited patiently as she listened to her sister open the door.

"Okay, it's quiet out here. What's up? Is everything okay?"

"Kind of?" Liv said, laughing slightly. "I have to be honest. This year has been challenging for me and I've thrown myself into my work—I know I told you guys that's why I haven't been able to spend a lot of time with everyone, but—" she sucked in a breath as her voice caught in her throat. Tears welled in her eyes, and she paused to compose herself.

"Tam, if I'm honest," she continued, her voice cracking with emotion, "I didn't want to face any of this. The fact that my marriage ended—and that it wasn't ever what I wanted it to be in the first place—that I don't have a family, that I'm basically starting from ground zero again when I thought I had this all figured out! I don't want to have to go through the dating thing again, worry about whether I'm finding the right person, do everything alone. I don't have friends like I had in college—when I met Connor, I let all of those relationships die out, I didn't make an effort."

"He didn't let you make an effort," Tamara corrected.

"True, but whatever," Liv sniffed. "There're so many unknowns, and it's all on me. If I screw this up again? Then what?"

Tamara was silent for a moment. "Liv," she said gently. "This has never been all on you. I know I haven't been the best about reaching out—I've been so busy with the kids and trying to figure out the whole mom thing...but it's no excuse. I think about you all the time, and I need to do better. You know how I've felt about Connor from the beginning—"

"I think that's why I avoided you guys, too. I knew you all thought I was being stupid—"

"But it doesn't matter," Tamara cut in. "I'm stupid all the time; we all are. I don't think this is your fault at all. You've always thought the best of people, and it's maddening that your optimism was taken advantage of."

Tears streamed down Liv's cheeks as she listened. "I've learned a lot," she said softly.

"I'm glad," Tamara said, emotion evident in her voice.

"I think I need help. I need someone to talk to. At work, I have teams for each project we take on, and," she sniffed, "this is a fairly big project for me."

"I'm on your team, babe. Just tell me what you need me to do," Tamara laughed.

Liv grinned. "I don't exactly know yet, but...maybe we can set up a regular time to talk? I could tell you what I'm working on? We could even do it on Marco Polo if it would be better for the timing to be flexible."

"Let me look at my calendar. Maybe we can find time on the weekend. I could go on a walk or something while we talk. And if it's for you, I won't have mom guilt over leaving the kids."

Liv laughed. "We could do it more frequently as needed," she teased.

"I love you, sis."

"Love you, too. See you soon."

Liv hung up the phone and stood up to search for a tissue.

15

Finished with work for the day, Liv walked into town toward City Hall. In the binder in the Cottage she'd seen an ad for the Sprucewood museum. It was free and open 'till four, the perfect little stop for late on a Tuesday afternoon. She approached the front of the house, pulled open the screen door, and stepped into a small entry. A guide walked toward her, smiling and beckoning her to come further down the hall.

"Welcome," the woman said, motioning at the room in front of her. "Have you been to the Sprucewood museum before?"

"Nope, first time," Liv grinned.

"Well you're in for a treat," the woman said, winking conspiratorially. "My name is Molly, and I'll be your guide today. We have four rooms—each one dedicated to one of the founding families of our beloved town..."

Liv listened as Molly dove into the history of Sprucewood, gazing at the pictures and artifacts displayed along the wall. Eugene Jones had moved here searching for gold, but ended up opening a trading post and staying put. He had eight children with two different women—his first wife died of a fever when she was only twenty-eight. Four kids by the age of twenty-eight. That even put Tamara to shame.

"...Eugene Jones founded our school, as well. Though it's much-expanded now, the original one-room schoolhouse is still in use."

Liv turned, her interest piqued. "Is that the only school in Sprucewood?"

"It is," Molly nodded.

"Huh. That's incredible that they still use it."

"Have you been over to see it?" Molly asked hopefully.

Liv shook her head. "No, but I have a friend who used to teach there."

"Oh!" Molly clapped her hands, delighted. "Who is it? Maybe I know them. My own kids all went there, and I've lived here for over thirty years."

"His name's Jonah—I don't know his last name, but he taught middle school."

Molly sighed, her face drawn into an expression of pity. "That poor man. He's a friend?"

Liv nodded.

"Then you know it wasn't his fault," Molly asserted passionately, pointing a finger at her.

Again, Liv nodded, not wanting to admit her complete lack of understanding.

"When they fired him—it wasn't right. He needed help, that's all," she said, muttering under her breath as she began walking, leading Liv into the next room. "You tell him Molly said hi. I hardly ever see him around town anymore. Though, I'm kind of a homebody to be honest," she said, turning and flashing an amused grin. "Now. This is the Cranston family," she began, pointing to a black and white portrait hanging next to the door.

Liv didn't hear much else from that moment on. Her

mind was spinning over what Molly'd said about Jonah. He'd been fired? It wasn't his fault? What was she talking about? She searched her memory of her conversations with him, attempting to find something that could give her a clue. At least now she felt validated that something hadn't been adding up when he'd talked about his life. Her intuition was right on. It wasn't any of her business...but when the tour ended, she casually decided that groceries for tonight could probably wait, and a meal at four-thirty in the afternoon wouldn't be the worst idea.

When she walked into Phil's, she immediately searched the bar area and found Bobby just where she'd hoped he'd be. She waved, and he motioned for her to join him.

"Hey there," he greeted her warmly. "Liv, right?"

"Good memory," she smiled, sitting on a stool in front of him.

"How've the last couple of days been?" he asked, hanging glasses above his head as he talked, the dishwasher still steaming next to him.

"Interesting," Liv said honestly, and Bobby laughed.

"That's how it should be, I guess. Boring isn't any fun," he grinned. "Can I get you anything?"

"Actually, yes. Can I order that BLT I was eyeing the other night?"

"Absolutely," he said, shifting to his left and typing on the monitor in front of him. "Fries, soup, or side salad?"

"Fries," she said without hesitation.

"You got it. What to drink?"

"Water is great."

Bobby reached for a glass, filled it halfway with ice, then pressed the button for water. He slid it to her, laughing at her alarm. The glass slid to a halt directly in front of her.

"I've gotten really good at getting glasses in the right place," he said.

Liv laughed and took a sip.

"So where's Jonah this afternoon. Working?"

"Probably," she said. "I had work today, and then I went to the museum just now. I haven't seen him."

"Hmmm," Bobby said, his eyes narrowing. "You went up to the springs with that group the other night?"

Liv nodded, taking a sip of water to avoid having to expound.

"It's beautiful up there," he said, eyeing her suspiciously.

"It is," she agreed. Looking down at the bar, she took a deep breath. "Bobby, can I ask...why isn't Jonah teaching anymore?"

Bobby placed both hands on the counter. "That," he sighed, "is a loaded question. Have you asked Jonah about it?"

Liv nodded. "He didn't say much. I'm not trying to pry; it's just—Molly said something down at the museum and I didn't want to bring it up with him, especially after—" she stopped short.

Bobby nodded, graciously ignoring her abrupt pause. "Why do you want to know?"

Liv searched for an answer. "I don't—I mean, I—" she stopped, her eyebrows furrowing. "I don't know," she admitted softly.

"Well, if it's just curiosity, then—"

"No, it's not," she quickly cut in. "At least, I don't think it is. I...think Jonah's a good guy, Bobby. I know that sounds silly because I've only been here a few days, but I can tell he's kind. And I'm coming from a really tough situation; it seems like he might be, too...maybe that's why I care. I feel connected to him in some way."

She looked at Bobby, searching his face for a response.

"Is that weird?" she asked, doubting herself when he remained quiet.

Bobby shook his head. "No, not weird. Jonah was an

excellent teacher. He lost his job because he had a drinking problem."

Liv looked puzzled. Drinking? "I haven't seen Jonah drink anything but water. Even at the springs—"

"He's been clean for over four years," Bobby clarified.

"Then why can't he go back to teaching? It seems like that's more than enough time—"

"No," Bobby said, moving closer. "Liv, it was awful. He made a lot of enemies in this town, and even though they're willing to interact with him themselves, it's another thing entirely for them to allow him back into the classroom with their children."

Liv's heart was pounding. She couldn't imagine Jonah doing anything that would alienate people like that.

"He's a good person, Liv. And he's been through a lot. I think you'll have to ask him about the rest, though. It's not my story to tell."

She nodded. "Thanks, Bobby."

"I'll go check on that BLT," he said, turning and walking back to the kitchen.

Liv wanted to wait and ask Jonah for his side of the story. She really did. But there was too much intrigue, and her curiosity got the better of her. Pulling out her phone, she typed Jonah's name into the Google search bar. She didn't know his last name, but she added the tags 'alcohol' and 'fired' along with 'Sprucewood' and 'teacher.' Within seconds, her finger hovered over the top hit. 'Teacher fired for alcohol-induced destructive rage, Sprucewood CO.'

The article was from 2014. She hesitated, not sure she wanted to read whatever disturbing information was in this text, but it was too tempting. She clicked the link and began to read.

. . .

'A male teacher at Sprucewood Middle School was fired this week after months-long investigations into accusations that he engaged in inappropriate behavior on school property.

A Golden County public spokeswoman confirmed that Jonah Wilson had been discharged but wouldn't comment further. Wilson hasn't responded to our inquiries, despite multiple messages seeking comment.

Wilson, who was Golden County's 2013 Teacher of the Year, was suspended without pay in September after arriving at the school inebriated and throwing a desk and attached chair through a closed window on the south side of the school. Witnesses say Wilson, after an altercation with another female staff member, "flew into a rage" and began to "throw school supplies around the room."

According to another staff member at Sprucewood Middle School (who preferred to remain anonymous), this was the third on-campus incident of Wilson's erratic behavior. "At this point, he's a safety issue for the staff, but more importantly, for the children he teaches. He needs help, and until he gets his drinking under control, he won't be allowed back onto school property."

"Here you go," Bobby said, and Liv frantically closed the screen even though she knew he couldn't see what she was looking at.

"Thanks. Looks delicious."

Bobby smiled and walked to the other end of the bar to help a man who had taken a seat while he'd been retrieving her meal. Liv picked up half of her sandwich and took a bite, the crisp lettuce and bacon a perfect compliment to the fluffy bread and sweet tomato. The deliciousness of the food did nothing to assuage her guilt at becoming an internet stalker.

What was she supposed to do now? Just pretend she didn't know? And how could he have done that? Drinking or no drinking, who would throw a desk out of a school window?

Liv swallowed, but the lump in her throat didn't go away. Was it possible to feel betrayed by someone you barely knew? She knew she was probably being overly dramatic, yet she couldn't shake the hurt and frustration.

'He's a good person,' Bobby had said, but in her experience, the road to being devalued and gaslighted was paved with 'good people' who 'only needed to get over' something or other. Mayonnaise squeezed out between the bread onto her lips as she took another bite, and she wiped it with her napkin. Maybe it was time she started looking at things realistically. Maybe it was time she stopped taking risks with her emotions at all.

16

Liv spent two days holed up in Holly Bough Cottage. She told herself it was because of the snowstorm that blew through Sprucewood, but her heart was difficult to convince. She'd gotten into a sort of routine: wake up around eight, field emails from Matt, eat lunch, work on a few mock-ups, then...Christmas movies. So many Christmas movies. After watching both *The Holiday* and *White Christmas* (after finishing *Love, Actually* and *A Christmas Proposal* the day before), Liv forced herself to get off the couch and take a shower. She was out of groceries and wasn't going to go into town looking like...well, like she'd sat on the couch and watched movies for two days straight.

Though she'd been stuck inside, she'd seen Jonah through the window going in and out of his cabin. What was it about him? Even after hearing that he wasn't exactly who she thought he was, she still couldn't stop thinking about him. Or staring after him as he walked across the property. She wanted to know his whole story, but after that night at the hot springs...

Turning off the hot water, she stepped onto the bathmat

and pulled a towel from the bar hanging on the wall next to the tub. She dried off, moisturized, and pulled on her warmest clothes—jeans, a sweater, wool socks—and dried her hair. It felt like a lot of effort to go through for a trip to the grocery store.

Though it probably would've been slightly warmer had she walked into town earlier, this way she'd be able to hear the carolers and see the lights. She needed a little real Christmas magic in her life instead of just watching it on television.

She shivered as she carefully navigated down the front steps and down the walkway when her feet suddenly shot out from under her. A shriek escaped her lips as she fell hard, landing on her tailbone. Tears collected in her eyes involuntarily as she lay on the cold cement in total shock.

"Liv?" a voice called in the distance, but she couldn't take a breath to speak.

"Liv?" the voice repeated, this time closer. Jonah's concerned face appeared above her, and she struggled to get up.

"Here," he said gently, sliding his hand underneath her head. "Lie still. Can you move your legs?"

She nodded, lifting her knees.

"Did you hit your head?"

"I don't think so," she said, her voice shaky. "Just hit my tailbone hard."

"Okay, I think it's probably safe to move you inside. Take my hand."

Jonah pulled her up, throwing her arm around his neck and holding her around the waist to support her weight.

"Let me get my key," she whispered as they stepped onto the porch. She fished in her pocket, wincing as she shifted her feet. Opening the door, Jonah helped her into the cottage and walked her to the couch.

"I'm going to get the carpet dirty," she said, looking down at her boots.

Jonah scoffed. "Lie down," he said, and she gingerly lowered herself to the cushions. Jonah quickly walked into the kitchen and pulled two grocery bags from under the sink, doubled them up, and filled them with a handful of ice.

"Here," he said, returning to the sofa and handing her the homemade ice pack.

"Thank you," she said, sliding it underneath her as he walked past the coffee table and pulled off her boots.

"Do you want to take off your coat?" he asked.

"I'm still freezing," she said, her teeth beginning to chatter.

"Probably just the shock of falling." He took a few steps and flicked the switch on the wall to turn on the fireplace.

Liv groaned. "I was trying to be so careful. How did you even see what happened?"

Jonah cleared his throat, hesitating. "I guess it was just the right time, right place kind of thing." He sat in the armchair next to the perpetually lit Christmas tree. "Where were you headed?"

"To get groceries. I'm out."

"Do you have a list? I could run into town and pick it up for you."

Liv smiled. "You don't have to do that."

"If you were desperate enough to walk into town in this weather, then it's likely you're probably on the brink of starvation."

Liv laughed and then winced in pain. "No jokes," she said, sucking in a breath. "It hurts too much."

"Sorry," Jonah grinned, and despite the pain, heat rose to Liv's cheeks as the lights from the tree glinted in his blue eyes.

"List?" he asked, breaking her daze.

"Right," she said, swallowing hard. "I wrote a few things on my phone—oh, is my purse still outside?"

"No, I grabbed it. It's on the table," he said, standing to retrieve it. He brought it to her, and she reached inside.

"Okay," she sighed. "Here it is. Salad kit if they have it, a dozen eggs, bread, lunch meat, cheese—I already have condiments—apples, and a couple of freezer pizzas or some other quick freezer meals." She set her phone on the table. "I didn't feel like cooking anything this week."

"Can you text that to me?" he asked, pulling out his cellphone. Liv copied and pasted the information into her phone and texted it to the number he gave her.

"It's the 21st," Jonah said, looking at his phone and then glancing at Liv. "Only four days 'till Christmas."

Liv nodded, then looked around the cottage and took a deep breath. Everything around her screamed holiday joy, but she couldn't feel it.

"Normally I'd be getting together with friends," he continued, "but given what happened the other night—"

"Jonah, don't ditch your friends on my account."

"It's not on your account; it's on account of Neil being a complete douchebag."

"Well. I'm sure others in that group would miss seeing you," she said, readjusting the ice under her lower back.

"Thanks for that."

Liv looked up to see a small smile playing at the corner of his mouth. She stifled a laugh. Was she flirting with him? Why was she lowering her guard when she knew what he'd done? Yes, he'd just rescued her from the front step, but that didn't change the fact that she didn't know whether she could trust him.

"For many reasons, I think I'm going to do my own thing this year," he said pointedly. "Do you have any plans?"

Her thoughts pushed for her to lie, to say she had plans to

avoid being alone with him again, but her mouth wouldn't listen. "Zero plans," she said. "Besides said freezer meals."

"That's kind of pathetic, don't you think?"

She scoffed, feigning offense. "I'm basically disabled, and you're mocking my Christmas plans?"

Jonah laughed. "I'm equal opportunity when it comes to my inappropriate comments."

"No jokes, remember?" Liv teased, and the anxiety she'd felt moments before seemed to seep out of her as she took in his amusement at her comments.

Jonah's smile faded and he looked at her intently. "Would you like to have Christmas dinner with me?" he asked simply.

Liv's heart-rate quickened, and suddenly, she couldn't feel the pain in her tailbone as acutely. She'd be alone again. With Jonah. Wasn't she supposed to avoid this? What was it the article had said? Fired for inappropriate behavior? Searching through the information she'd accrued, she attempted to muster her prior concern, but looking at his kind eyes and soft expression, she just couldn't see any part of him that could be considered a threat.

"I'd love to," she said softly.

Jonah smiled. "Okay, then. I'll go get your groceries."

"You don't need—"

"Just rest," he said, brushing his hand against hers as he stood and walked past her toward the door. Her skin tingled, and she had to remind herself to breathe.

"Wait, do you want me to turn on a Christmas movie for you?" he asked from behind the sofa.

"Will you mock me if I say yes?"

Jonah chuckled and walked toward the TV. When he turned it on, he saw it was already on the Hallmark channel. Liv grinned as he rolled his eyes.

"Thanks," she said, then watched him wave as he walked out the door.

17

Liv opened her eyes to noise in the kitchen and jumped, then groaned when pain exploded in her back.

"Hey," Jonah said, concern in his voice. "I'm sorry, I didn't mean to wake you."

"How long have I been out?" she asked groggily, noticing her movie still playing on the television.

"I was gone at the store for about forty minutes, so...I have no idea," Jonah laughed, his face peering over the couch. "Are you sure you didn't hit your head?"

"I'm sure."

They stared at each other a moment, then Jonah cleared his throat. "I picked up everything on your list and some things for Christmas dinner. I wondered...would you want to make dinner at my house?"

"Your cottage?"

He shook his head. "No, my actual house. I've got a larger kitchen over there and, more importantly, a smoker."

She raised an eyebrow. "You cook?"

"I smoke meat. There's a difference," he grinned. "I could just smoke it and bring it over if you'd rather—"

"No," Liv smiled. "That would be fun to cook over there. Full disclosure: I'm not an amazing chef. I've done parts of Christmas dinner before, but in New York, we usually had it catered—" She stopped short, the image of her, Connor, and his friends gathered around the table while she attempted to play hostess. Always coming up short.

"Liv? Are you alright?" Jonah asked gently.

She took a deep breath. "I think so," she sighed. "This time of year is hard for me."

Jonah's jaw clenched, and she saw something pass across his face. "Me, too." He cleared his throat. "All of your groceries are put away," he said, meeting her eyes. "Do you need anything else tonight?"

Liv looked up at him, and her heart ached to pull him close. Her mind spun with warnings, rationality, and hesitation, but it didn't seem to matter.

"Do you want to watch a movie with me tonight? And eat something ridiculously unhealthy? It doesn't have to be a Christmas movie; we could watch whatever."

Jonah raised an eyebrow. "I'm not normally a movie kind of guy," he said slowly, and Liv's heart sunk. "But," he continued, "if it's not cheesy, I guess it's the least I could do for an invalid like yourself."

Liv smiled, attempting to mask her excitement.

"And I might have gotten a pint of Ben and Jerry's at the store."

"You did?"

Jonah laughed at her wide-eyed expression. "It was supposed to be a surprise."

"It is. The best surprise," she grinned.

Jonah walked back into the kitchen, and Liv could hear him rifling around for what she assumed were bowls, spoons, and an ice cream scoop. She reached for the remote sitting on the coffee table and navigated to the TV guide, looking for movie options. Eventually, Jonah appeared beside her with two full bowls in his hands.

"I can sit up and use these pillows—"

"No," Jonah interrupted. "Just lift your legs." He set the bowls on the table, and she lifted her legs obediently, supporting her lower back with her hands on either side of her bruised tailbone. Jonah sat on the couch, and she lowered her legs on top of his lap.

"Is that weird?" he asked, reaching for the bowls and handing her one.

She shook her head, taking a bite of ice cream. Handing him the remote, she said, "You choose."

Liv forced herself to take a deep breath and regulate her nerves before she started shivering. She still had her coat on, and that helped, but she was losing her mind with him being so close. What had gotten into her? Yes, he was incredibly cute, and yes, he had been extremely kind to her, but what about the other night? He said he didn't want to talk about things with someone he barely knew. She was that person. He barely knew her, and she barely knew him. And the things she did know should be enough of a red flag to make her take precautions. Like not being alone with him in her cottage late at night.

But was that all she knew about him? That was third-party information. Everything she'd seen personally had been sweet. Kind. Considerate. But she also knew she had a propensity for falling for people who knew how to be captivating, sweet, and kind...until they weren't.

"How do you feel about Million Dollar Baby?" Jonah asked.

"Sounds perfect."

Maybe she was falling into another trap, but right now, she couldn't force herself to care.

Liv woke the next morning and persuaded herself to get up and out of bed. Walking felt like torture. She turned around to take a look at her bruise in the mirror. She grimaced at the dark blue and purple splaying out across the skin of her lower back. Popping two extra-strength ibuprofen pills into her mouth, she took a drink of water from the tap.

She grinned, thinking about last night. The movie wasn't a holiday romance by a long shot, but the ending had been surprisingly heart-wrenching. Though she'd tried to hide her emotion as the credits rolled, she hadn't been completely successful. But, she could've sworn Jonah's eyes had been shimmering when he caught her wiping away a tear, so at least she hadn't been the only one.

Walking into the kitchen, she pulled out a frying pan and turned on the medium burner on the stove. She pulled two eggs from the fridge and cracked them into a bowl, then scrambled them with a fork. Greasing the pan with a stick of butter, she poured the eggs into the pan and dusted them with salt and pepper. She toasted a slice of bread while they cooked, then gingerly sat down at the kitchen table with her plate.

Taking a bite, she opened her laptop and clicked on Messenger.

Hey. I think operation handsome guy might be back on.

Sara's icon showed as active, so Liv watched for her to respond while she ate.

. . .

>*I need details.*

😄 *There aren't really details, per se, but he may have helped me last night when I slipped. And invited me to Christmas dinner.*

>*Did you kiss?*

No! Sara, I barely met this guy!

>*And??*

Focus. I need your help on this. I found out randomly (through some people in town...and possibly a Google search) that he got fired because of a drinking problem.

>*How recent?*

As far as I know, the drinking stopped a few years ago.

>*Have you asked him about it?*

No! He doesn't even know that I know, so how would I even bring that up? Like "hey, I was stalking you in town and heard you used to be alcoholic and you threw a desk out of a school window. Tell me about that."

. . .

>*He threw a desk out of a school window? Yikes.*

I know.

>*But I mean, you wouldn't have to say it like that.* 😂

I don't know what to do, Sara. I really like this guy. I know I barely know him, but it's like I'm...drawn to him. But in the past, the guys I've been drawn to have been like Connor. What if he's another Connor!? I have literal proof that he might be. I'm worried I can't trust myself, which...what does that mean!? I'll never be able to meet a good guy because I'm obviously only attracted to guys with issues?

>*Ok, back up a sec. Does this guy do anything like Connor does?*

No. He's literally his opposite, I think. He's more reserved. Doesn't seem to care much about what people think of him. Obviously has some history he's not talking about, though...

>*But if he's a nice guy, it seems like he's probably worked through whatever it was.*

That's what I was thinking, too! But...I don't know. Maybe I'm a horrible judge of character.

. . .

>*Don't you think you figured out what to NOT look for after Connor? And Liv...you're only there for a short time. It's not like you're going to marry the guy.*

No, I know. But if I get involved...I don't know if I can handle really liking him and then never seeing him again. Not so soon after everything else.

>*But don't you already really like him?*

Good point.

>*It's already going to suck to leave. Might as well make-out.*

You're a terrible influence.

>*You're welcome. Now I actually have to work.*

Thanks for talking me off the ledge.

>*Anytime* 🩶

A thought occurred to Liv as she closed her computer. It *was* already going to suck to leave. And she wasn't guaranteed to have any closure in this situation anyway. He was clearly feeling just as alone as she was, so maybe he only wanted someone to be around and wasn't actually attracted to her. And even if he was...if she asked him about his past, either way it would be a partial win for her. Either he'd get upset and it would be easier to walk away from this place or he'd explain things and she wouldn't have to wonder anymore.

She finished her breakfast and as she placed her dishes in the sink, then reached for her phone on the counter. She realized she had Jonah's number. She'd texted him her grocery list last night. Scrolling to find the message, she clicked on it and began to type.

Hey! Are you home right now?

Her finger hit the 'send' button and she instantly regretted it. What was she going to do now!? Go over and say what exactly?

I am. What's up?

What was up? Liv had no clue where to go from here, but she knew she needed answers. She'd spent too much time trying to please people and ignoring her own emotional needs in a relationship. What was a relationship worth if she wasn't comfortable in it?

Without texting back, she found her outdoor gear and got dressed. The medicine had kicked in and she felt almost normal for the time being, though her back was definitely still stiff. She knew she'd feel it later, but enjoyed the relief for the moment. Stepping into the cold, she realized she hadn't done anything to make herself look presentable. She hesi-tated—her hand holding the cold metal of the doorknob—but then closed the door and held on to the railing as she descended the steps.

The ice was cleared at this point, but she could see where she'd likely slipped. A low puddle of water sat in a dip in the concrete, shimmering in the sunlight. She splashed it with her boot as she passed.

Jonah opened the door before she knocked. He must have seen her walking toward his cottage.

"Hey," he greeted her.

"Hey."

"Want to come in?"

"Sure," she said, stepping past him and wiping her boots on the mat.

"How are you feeling today?"

"I'm hopped up on meds, so pretty good," she laughed. "I wanted to—"

Jonah held up a finger as he pulled his phone from his pocket. "Hello?" he said, answering it. "Oh, sure. Which one?" His eyebrows furrowed as he listened. "No problem. I'll head over in a minute. Yep. Thanks." He hung up the phone and Liv looked at him questioningly.

"Leaking faucet on the outside of the gift shop."

"Do you need to go now?" she asked.

"I should, but what did you need?"

"Oh, nothing, I just wanted to talk for a second. We can—"

"Do you want to walk with me? It won't be a long repair. But I understand if you'd rather not be out in the cold," he shrugged.

"No, that's great," Liv said. "My hat's in my pocket if I get cold."

Jonah nodded, pulling his coat on and grabbing his

toolbox sitting next to the door.

"I haven't even been to the gift shop yet," Liv said as they walked outside. "Is there good stuff in there?"

"If you're looking for souvenirs, sure," he said. "But I honestly haven't been in there recently."

Liv's heart started to pound, and she mustered her courage. "Jonah, the reason I came by today is that I wanted to ask you about something. I was at the museum in town, and I met Molly—"

"She's such a sweet lady," Jonah said, smiling.

"She really is. I mentioned that I knew you and she said something about how I must know that 'all that' wasn't your fault."

Jonah stared straight ahead, and Liv pressed on. "I obviously didn't know what she was talking about, so...I asked Bobby when I stopped there for lunch."

She looked at Jonah to gauge his reaction, but his face was stoic. "I don't want to pry, but—" she took a deep breath, "I also really enjoy hanging out with you. Given my history, I'm just nervous...it's hard for me to make friends in general because it's hard for me to trust people, but especially guys." Guys I'm attracted to, she thought but didn't say it.

They reached the side of the building, and Jonah led her around the north side. They found the faucet and saw drips of water dropping onto the ground below it. Jonah squatted down next to it and opened his toolbox.

"And I know we barely know each other and that I'm only here for two weeks, so if bringing this up offends you, I'm sorry," she said, her voice losing steam with every word.

Jonah used a screwdriver to look inside the housing. "It doesn't offend me," he said. "It's just kind of embarrassing."

"Trust me; I'm the last person who's going to judge you."

Jonah pulled a new piece of something from the bottom of his toolbox. "I had a drinking problem. Which was obviously not ideal for a teacher. When it became a liability, I lost my job. And my wife."

"That's why you said it was your fault."

Jonah nodded, breathing hard as he worked with his wrench to remove something Liv didn't recognize from the pipe protruding from the wall.

"We were only married for two years."

"How did it start? The drinking?"

Jonah shrugged but didn't answer.

"Do you still struggle with it?" Liv asked.

"I struggle with plenty of things in life, but drinking isn't one of them. That was a wake-up call for me, and I haven't had a drop in four years. But I'm not naive enough to think that it couldn't be a problem again in the future. I have pretty strict rules I follow."

"That's impressive. I've never been a drinker, but I've heard it's not easy to quit."

Jonah shook his head. "I should've quit sooner."

Liv hesitated, not sure what to say to that. "You never returned to teaching?" she asked, changing the subject.

"I didn't really have the option," he admitted. "Unless I moved to a new town. But I love it up here. I own my house outright. A teacher's salary wouldn't compensate for the lack of a mortgage somewhere else."

"Why not commute?"

"I'm not the commuting type."

Jonah attached the new piece and replaced the faucet, pulling the screws from his pocket.

"Where's your ex now?" Liv asked.

"I'm not sure. We haven't talked in years," Jonah said, standing up, then wiping his hands on his jeans.

"I'm sorry," Liv said.

Jonah picked up his toolbox, and Liv walked next to him back toward their cottages.

"This place is magical," she said. "They advertised it online as being a place where 'hopes would be renewed.'"

Jonah grinned, raising an eyebrow.

"I know, it sounds cheesy. But I think it's working for me."

"What hopes have been renewed since you've been here?" Jonah asked, and Liv playfully smacked his arm. "No, I'm serious," he laughed.

Liv exhaled slowly, tucking her hands in her coat pockets. "The last year I've wondered if I'd ever be able to feel like myself again. I think I still have a lot of work to do—to be honest with myself and the people I love so I can heal. I feel hopeful about that. It's too bad it took me so long to finally make some progress."

They approached Jonah's door, and his pace slowed. "It's been three years. And I think I'm exactly where I left off," he mused.

"It sounds like you've made some significant progress."

"Not really," he shook his head. "I'm not drinking anymore, but nothing has changed here," he said, motioning to his chest. "I've just figured out how to live with it."

Liv's heart ached, taking in his pained expression. He must have really loved her. Without thinking, she stepped closer and wrapped her arms around him, laying her head on his chest. Hesitantly, Jonah returned the embrace. She breathed in the smell of his clean cotton shirt and heard the beating of his heart.

Stepping back, she smiled. "Thanks for talking."

"Anytime," he said, turning to open his door.

"Hey, I made an appointment in Golden this afternoon. I wanted to connect with a designer I've heard great things about; she's based there, and the office is closed from the twenty-third through the new year. I was planning to catch an Uber, but I wondered...would you like to come with me?"

"Are you using me for my transportation?" he teased.

"One-hundred percent."

Jonah laughed. "What time?"

"We'd need to leave here around three-thirty. The appointment itself should be fairly quick," she said.

"Let me make a call. I'll see what I can do."

Liv nodded. "Sounds good. Text when you know?" She smiled, her heart light as she walked to her door. Her eyes took in the holiday decor outside the cabin as she approached, seeing it differently than she had when she first arrived. Finally, it was beginning to feel a lot like Christmas.

18

L iv heard Jonah's truck idling on the street outside around three twenty-five. She hustled to finish braiding her hair and apply lip gloss, then ran out and gingerly lifted herself into the passenger seat. The fact that he opened up during their chat had lifted a burden from her shoulders. She knew Sara was right: this likely wasn't a relationship that would go anywhere beyond the next week. Not even a week. Five days. That's all she had left. But it still felt good to be on equal ground.

"Where to?" Jonah asked, his dimple in full view as he smiled, placing his hands on the steering wheel.

"I've got it pulled up here," she said, opening her maps app on her phone. "Basically, just go into Golden, and I'll direct you from there."

Jonah nodded, pulling away from the curb. Five days. If this was just supposed to be a fun, random connection she'd made on vacation, why did she dread leaving so much? Especially since she was actually excited—for the first time in months—to spend time with her sister. She breathed deeply, attempting to keep her eyes trained ahead of her out the windshield. This sense of connection probably had more to do with finally talking with someone who had as much baggage as she did. She needed like-minded people, that's all.

She reached over and turned up the volume on the radio.

"I love this song," she explained, and Jonah laughed as she started mouthing the words to 'Romeo and Juliet' by Taylor Swift.

"I've never heard this song."

"Are you serious? Have you been living under a rock?" Liv teased, becoming more animated by the second.

"I can count on one hand the number of times I've listened to the radio in the last year," Jonah defended himself.

"So why was it on today?" she asked, raising an eyebrow while continuing to lip-sync the chorus.

"I knew we were driving for a while, and I thought—I didn't know—" he blushed, stumbling over his words, and Liv couldn't handle how adorable he looked. "—if you would want music or not."

"I always want music," she said, settling into her seat as the song ended. "What's your favorite music to listen to?"

Jonah sobered at the question, and Liv turned the volume down as advertisements began blasting through the speakers.

"Ever since—" he shook his head. "I don't listen to music much anymore."

Liv studied his face. What was he still holding back? The fact that he closed up at certain points in every conversation didn't escape her and, while she wasn't concerned that he was dangerous, she desperately wanted to be the person he chose to be open with.

They sat in silence, and Liv could feel the pull of her past —the desire to make herself into whatever someone else wanted or needed so that she could feel wanted and needed. But with Jonah...it all felt different. And terrifying. It wasn't obvious what would make him want her, and the insecurity that fueled in her was staggering.

At the same time, this was the moment that made her acutely aware of her own lack of self-knowledge. What would Liv do in this situation? Not 'what would Jonah want her to do,' but what would be true to her own soul? She didn't know that either.

"I don't know myself," she whispered, her eyes stinging.

"Hmm?"

Her heart hammered in her chest. "I don't know myself," she said a little louder, and Jonah pressed the volume button, turning the radio off entirely.

"What do you mean?" he asked.

"I mean—I'm sitting here and...I don't know how to act. I'm so used to doing things or saying things to make someone else like me or to put on a good face, and I have no clue what *I* want."

Jonah turned, his eyes meeting hers for a moment before his attention shifted back to the road.

"It's like I'm just a shell. Moving through space, you know? Waiting to be filled by someone else's expectations, and when I don't have those...I'm just...empty."

Jonah nodded. "Emptiness is a feeling I've become accustomed to."

"Not me," she laughed mirthlessly. "I don't know what to do with this. I've always had something else—someone else— to tell me how to feel or what to do. Where do I even go from here?"

"I think," he started, then paused. "It doesn't matter what I think," he scoffed.

"It does—"

"No, it doesn't," he said more forcefully. "Because I don't take my own advice."

Liv stared at the side of his face. His five o'clock shadow

over his strong jaw, his dark hair curling around his ears, and the band of his worn baseball cap. His hand sat on the seat next to him, and her hand slid over his rough fingers. The warmth of his skin surprised her and sent tingles up her wrist and arm.

"I still want to hear it," she whispered. She watched as his chest lifted and fell, then held her breath as his hand turned over and enclosed around her own.

"I think you need to experiment. Try a bunch of new things, even if they sound crazy or like too much effort, just so you can start to understand what makes you happy."

Liv nodded. "And just accept that it's going to take a while," she added. "Just like getting to know someone new." She laughed.

"What?" Jonah asked, a smile playing at the corner of his mouth.

"It's like—" she started, but then began laughing so hard that she couldn't get the words out. Her stomach muscles began to ache, and she gasped for breath. "I'm sorry," she squeaked. "It's like—I'm dating myself!"

"And why is that so funny?" Jonah asked, amused.

"I don't know!" she said, finally taking a breath and wiping the tears from her eyes with her free hand. "It just hit me. It's hilarious. And pathetic."

Jonah chuckled. "You're weird. I can tell you that already," he teased. "And I need directions." He lifted his hand from hers and pointed at their exit.

"Oh, right," she said, composing herself. "Take a left, and then we'll take the third right on Johnson Rd."

They exited, and Jonah followed her directions until they parked on the street in front of a round sign with swoopy letters spelling out 'AerieDesign.'

"Want to come in with me?" Liv asked, and Jonah nodded. As she opened the door, his voice made her pause.

"Liv," he said, and she turned toward him. "It's brave."

She soaked in the intensity of his gaze and nodded, then stepped out onto the curb.

When they returned to the truck forty-five minutes later, Liv's mind was buzzing with ideas and inspiration. She frantically wrote on her tablet, attempting to note every new thought that had occurred to her during the appointment.

"So, this is what you do for a living?" Jonah asked, putting the keys in the ignition.

"Yep," she said, still distracted. "I'm quite good at being a designer. Less good at being a business owner," she sighed. "I need to find a way to be more organized so that I can be a better leader. If I ever lost my team, I'd be sunk."

"How long have your employees worked for you?" Jonah asked, pulling back onto the highway.

"Two years?" Liv questioned. "Almost three, actually. Which means I have a great opportunity to learn new skills right now, before anything in their lives change, and while our day-to-day operations are seamless. But of course...my life hasn't been seamless this past year. I didn't have any extra energy to work on management skills."

"I get that," Jonah said. "But I don't have any excuse."

Liv turned toward him in her seat. "Do you have things you'd like to do?"

"What do you mean?"

"Well, you talked about not taking your own advice, and now you just said you don't have any excuse. For what? Do you want to do something new and haven't been able to do it?" When Jonah was silent, Liv continued, "No judgment. I was only curious."

"No, it's okay," he said, "I'm just thinking. The short

answer is yes. But I don't think I've let myself think about any of my own dreams for a long time."

Liv found herself watching him again, wondering what was going on in his head.

"Can I show you something?" he asked, his voice barely a whisper.

"Sure."

Jonah didn't explain, and Liv sat silently, watching the road as he took the Sprucewood exit, but then turned in the opposite direction of the cabin. After passing the buildings in town, they wound through the trees on a road packed with snow, eventually stopping in front of tall iron gates. The sign above them read "Sprucewood Cemetery," and Liv suppressed the questions that were on the tip of her tongue, waiting for Jonah to speak.

He didn't. Slowly, he pulled the keys from the ignition and opened his car door. She followed, stepping out into the snow next to the road, grateful she'd worn her real boots. Jonah walked under the gates, pausing briefly for her to join him. As they stepped in silence along the main path, Liv read the headstones of the graves they passed. Each name seemed to strike a chord within her; she'd never lost anyone close to her, not even her grandparents. She didn't know what this kind of loss felt like.

They turned left, then right, and eventually slowed next to a petite granite headstone. A breeze whispered through the trees, shaking snow loose from the branches and brushing their cheeks with winter chill. Jonah hunched, his hands shoved into his coat pockets as Liv stopped next to him. Her eyes took in the information on the headstone.

Oliver Wilson, November 2011-February 2012.
If love could have saved you, you would have lived forever.

Wilson. That was Jonah's last name in the article she'd read. But that meant—

"This is my son," Jonah whispered, his breath lifting into the cold air like smoke.

Liv was speechless.

"He died of SIDS. Claire—my ex-wife—was insistent there hadn't been anything in the crib with him. I was at work when it happened. We didn't have any of the normal risk factors..." he trailed off, looking down and rocking lightly on his feet in the packed snow.

"Jonah, I'm so sorry," Liv breathed. Images raced through her brain; even though she had no idea what Claire looked like, she envisioned her walking into Oliver's room with a smile, reaching into the crib to wake him since he'd been sleeping so long...

Jonah exhaled. "If I would've known that I'd seen him for the last time when I left for work that morning—"

"You couldn't have known," Liv said, tears filling her eyes as she watched Jonah's face twist in anguish. "You couldn't have known," she repeated, closing the space between them and wrapping her arms around him.

She felt his body shaking as he cried, and her mind raced to connect the dots. 2012. That was before he was fired from his teaching job. *He lost a child after only three months of being a father*. Tears streamed down her cheeks as she held him.

After a few moments, Jonah's breathing returned to normal, and Liv stepped back, lifting her eyes to his. She wanted to speak. To say something profound that would somehow make this all better and undo the past. Instead, she simply looked at him, attempting to communicate all her good intentions without the needed words to bring them to life. Jonah simply nodded. Taking one last forlorn glance at the headstone, he reached for Liv's hand and pulled her back toward the entrance.

Back inside his truck, Jonah pulled a u-turn and headed back toward town. Liv rubbed her hands together, anticipating the warm air that should be coming out of the vents any moment.

"Why did you take me there?" Liv asked. "I'm grateful you did," she added, "I was just wondering."

Jonah cleared his throat. "I usually don't mind when people hear about my past and make assumptions about me. And I'm not making excuses for my behavior back then, but —" he stopped short, thinking. "I guess it kind of sounds like I'm about to make an excuse."

"No, I don't see it like that," Liv assured him, waiting for him to continue.

"Looking back, I feel sad for myself when Oliver died. Claire and I had only been married for six months when she got pregnant. We were young and neither of us had family living close. We had good friends, but somehow...being with them after—it made it worse."

They turned onto Pine Street, driving past Phil's toward the Cottages. Liv held her hands up into the stream of hot air that was now rushing into the cab.

"Claire started going out all the time. Distracting herself. She resented me for wanting to stay home, but after a day of teaching, the last thing I wanted to do was talk to people."

Liv nodded, doing her best to show him that she was an avid and engaged listener.

"It felt like a dark cloud was always over me. I couldn't shake it. And then, one night I went out with her—she wouldn't lay off me, and I figured if I made an effort, it would show her that I was trying."

The truck pulled along the road to their cottages, and Liv

was already frustrated that they'd only have a few more minutes to talk.

"It was that night that I..." he parked the car in front of the path to Holly Bough Cottage and ran his hands over his face in exhaustion. "I drank too much. And it felt like such a relief. I could escape. I think I had fun, but that part didn't matter. The only thing I cared about was not feeling that black hole inside of me every day," he explained, motioning to his chest. "It was an easier way out."

Liv nodded, taking off her seatbelt and turning in her seat. "It makes complete sense," she said. "I can't imagine how hard that must've been."

Jonah gave a sardonic laugh, fiddling with his keys. "That's the thing; once I started drinking, nothing was hard. Everything felt easy and doable. I didn't listen when people started telling me I had a problem. I had finally found something that made me feel good, and everyone was trying to take it away from me." He placed his hands again on the steering wheel, then dropped them to the seat and met her eyes.

"Then Claire left me. And I got fired. All in the same week. That was when I got serious about quitting, but it took me a little time to be successful."

Liv watched his face, the honesty and vulnerability wonderful but also slightly overwhelming.

"I guess that's a long way of saying I showed you this because...I care what you think."

Liv felt heat rising up her neck and into her cheeks, and the air seemed to thicken with his words.

Jonah took a deep breath and continued. "I didn't like the idea of you thinking I was...I don't know. Someone dangerous."

"The stories I've seen from that time don't even seem like you," Liv said. "I can't imagine you—" she stopped short, realizing she'd come close to exposing her internet search history.

"I asked you about all of that because I cared about the answer. I needed to know you weren't another one of *those* guys."

Jonah looked at her quizzically.

"You know, the guys who are charming and handsome at first, but then you find yourself listening to them talk about themselves for hours over dinner—never once taking advantage of a break in conversation to ask a personal question about you. And how they downplay their issues and baggage, insisting it's all in the past...but then you catch them with another woman inside a cafe as you're walking to work—"

"Theoretically," Jonah said, his eyes trained on hers.

"Right. Theoretically."

He sighed. "I understand if all of this is a little much. And I'm not going to pretend like that 'baggage' is over for me. It's not. I still feel sad a lot, and I have to try not to numb it every day. I get it if I'm not a guy you're interested in."

Liv's heart skipped a beat. "Do you want me to be interested in you?" she asked, surprising even herself with her gumption.

"I—I don't want you to be anything you're not; I just thought—"

"Are you interested in me?"

Jonah paused, looking out his window, and Liv held her breath. When he turned back toward her, she could tell he was nervous. His gaze shifted between her, the dashboard, and the windshield, not able to lock on any one thing for more than a few seconds. His hands shook, and he cleared his throat one too many times.

After a moment, he reached down and unclicked his buckle, then shifted into the middle bench seat and finally looked directly at her. It was as if he held her attention in some sort of magnetic field; even if she'd wanted to, she wouldn't have been able to glance away. The rough fingers of his left hand grazed her cheek as he reached up to tuck an errant piece of hair behind her ear, leaving behind a trail of electric heat above her jawline.

"Can I—" he started, his voice low, but before he could finish, Liv was already nodding her head. With agonizingly slow movement, he closed the gap between them. Just before it felt like Liv's heart was about to explode with anticipation, his hand slipped around her waist and pulled her close, his lips finally meeting hers.

He kissed her gently—tenderly, and Liv was intent on enjoying every second. This was how a first kiss was supposed to be. Soft, questioning. Ebullient, yet still tantalizingly guarded. Her fingers traced his jaw and neck, playing with the unruly curls around his left ear. In this moment, Liv had no problem recognizing what her heart wanted.

19

Liv waved goodnight to Jonah with an exuberant smile on her face as she ascended the steps to her cottage. Opening the doors to holly garland, Christmas villages, and a new plate of fresh cookies on the table felt anything but over-the-top tonight. Instead, it was the perfect magical background for what had just transpired in her world. She had been kissed. By a really decent guy. The fact that he opened up to her made her more optimistic than ever that he wasn't anything like Connor. Or Neil, for that matter. Which meant...she was capable of attracting a cute guy who *wasn't* a creep.

This fact alone lifted her spirits exponentially. Hope was something she hadn't felt a lot of over the last year, but this evening with Jonah? All of it served to reignite a positivity about her future she didn't think existed anymore.

As she brushed her teeth, the kiss played over and over in her mind. How he smelled faintly of sandalwood, how the collar on his jacket brushed her ear, how his hand pressed gently on the small of her back—

She took a deep breath and looked in the mirror. Even

with toothpaste in her mouth, she couldn't stop smiling. Spitting, she took a drink of water and splashed more on her face. Barely taking the time to dry her skin, she rushed into her bedroom to cozy up on her bed and triumphantly message Sara.

Liv woke on the twenty-third of December to choirs of angels. From somewhere on the grounds, beautiful chords of Christmas classics rang out, making their way through her windows and joyously welcoming her to one of the best mornings of her life. Jonah had kissed her last night, and she'd slept like a baby to boot.

Jumping out of bed, she raced first to the bathroom, then to the kitchen to make breakfast. Cracking two eggs in a liquid measuring cup, she pulled a frying pan from the cupboard and began heating it on the stove. She scrambled the eggs and toasted a piece of bread, then spread peanut butter and jam across the crisp surface before putting everything on a plate and walking to the table.

She opened a window slightly to better hear the music, then ate her breakfast in absolute peace. Only when she finished did she pick up her phone, grinning as she saw two text messages from Jonah. Quickly placing her dishes in the sink, she walked into the living room and sat on the sofa to read them.

>*Good morning. Do you have plans today? I have the day off, barring an emergency of some sort.*

Hey. The only plans I have are with you 😄

. . .

Too much? She questioned herself, but then sent the message anyway, reminding herself that he'd been the one to make the first move.

>*Sleigh ride at noon? They're going up around the other side of the farm (so you won't be bored by the same old scenery from last time).*

Sounds perfect. Do we need to go early?

>*Meet me outside around eleven-thirty.*

I'll be there.

She looked at the clock. It was already past ten, which meant she needed to shower and get ready ASAP. Taking her time, she enjoyed the process of preparing for an exciting event. Even though they'd gotten close last night, she knew how different it was to see each other in the light of day...and not in a cozy truck on a cold, dark, emotionally charged evening. She meticulously dried her hair and didn't pull it up since she knew she'd likely be wearing a beanie.

Grabbing a couple of snacks for the road, she slipped into her coat and boots, wrapped her scarf around her neck, and stepped outside. She immediately found Jonah standing in front of his door waiting, and her heart leaped.

"Hi," he said with a smile as she walked within earshot.

"Hey," she answered, walking straight up to him and giving him a hug.

He held her tightly and she breathed him in. As she

stepped back, he reached for her hand and began leading her toward the sleigh rides.

"Are you needed for maintenance this morning?" she asked, and Jonah laughed. "What?" she prodded, looking at him quizzically.

"Can I admit something to you?"

Liv nodded.

"It sounds really pathetic, but...I kind of made up that maintenance thing."

Liv's brow furrowed.

"Not everything," he hastened to clarify, "I do maintenance on those sleighs all the time, but I'm not required to ride along."

She raised an eyebrow. "Are you saying you lied to get me to go on that first sleigh ride with you?"

Jonah nodded sheepishly. "I did. I wanted to have time to talk with you, but I couldn't think of a way to set it up without seeming—"

"Desperate?"

He nudged her. "I was going to say overly enthusiastic. I'm sorry I coerced you into going with me."

Liv took a deep breath. "Can I tell you something?"

"Do I want to know?" Jonah asked, his eyes narrowing.

"I might've internet stalked you," she admitted.

Jonah's smile faded, and Liv continued. "I know I shouldn't have, but I was so curious. And I still asked you about everything—"

"No, you don't need to apologize," he said, letting out a breath. "It's public information. But I hate that *that's* what people see when they Google me. And of course, reporters never tell the full story."

Liv nodded. "I'm sorry."

"Are we even?" Jonah teased good-humoredly.

"Even," she laughed, grateful to have it out in the open.

"So. Christmas dinner."

"What about it?" Liv asked, tucking her free hand into her coat pocket to keep warm.

"We know I'm doing the turkey, but what else should we make?"

"Hmmm. I love sweet potatoes and cornbread stuffing. Those are my must-haves," Liv answered, her mouth practically watering just thinking about her favorite dishes. "What about you?"

"Deviled eggs. And pumpkin pie."

"I could get on board with both of those."

Jonah didn't answer, and Liv felt him stiffen next to her. She followed his gaze to the queue for the sleigh rides and saw the catalyst for his sudden disengagement from their conversation.

"Hey!" Paige called, waving to them from the line. Neil, Krista, and Ryan stood next to her. She motioned for them to come join their group, and Jonah hesitantly acquiesced, dropping Liv's hand as they walked closer.

"Are you guys taking a ride? We can all sit together," Paige offered, eyeing Liv appraisingly.

"It seems like they're together," Neil smirked. "Not sure they want more company."

Paige reached out and punched his arm. "They're not together," she scoffed, but then quieted when she caught a slight blush on Liv's cheeks. "You guys are fine riding all together, right?"

Liv nodded, attempting to save Jonah any awkwardness with his friends. "Sure, the more the merrier," she said, forcing a smile to her lips.

"Great. We've been trying to get in touch about Christmas dinner," she said, turning her attention to Jonah. "Did you lose your phone or something?"

Jonah shook his head. "I think I'm going to do my own thing."

"When did that happen? I thought we talked about this last week," Paige said, obviously confused.

"After that night at the hot springs," Jonah said slowly, looking pointedly at Neil, "it felt like I needed a break."

Paige and Krista looked between the two men but didn't say anything.

"We've been pretty busy lately; this season's been nuts," Ryan said, attempting to diffuse the awkwardness. "How've you been doing, Liv?"

"Good," she grinned, thankful for the change of subject. "Just working and watching a lot of Christmas movies."

"I love Christmas movies," Krista sighed. "I haven't had time to watch any yet, though."

The line began to move forward as people boarded. When it was their turn, they took the ends of two benches in the middle of the sleigh. Liv slid in first, followed by Jonah. She grimaced when Paige squished in on the other side of him. This wasn't exactly what she'd been hoping for when he'd asked her to go on a ride with him, and she had to physically stop herself from jumping up and pushing past people to get off and run home.

This time, when the flannel blankets came around, Paige grabbed one and spread it over her and Jonah's lap, leaving Liv to bundle up on her own.

"Do you remember when we did this last year?" Paige said, laughing and nudging Jonah's shoulder.

"Don't remind me," Krista groaned, turning her body to look at her friend behind her. "I felt like a complete third wheel."

The safety announcement sounded from the driver, but nobody in this group paid him any attention. They did, at least, lower their voices.

"Whatever, I was single, too," Ryan said, turning sideways on his seat.

"So we were both third wheels," she laughed.

"Fifth and sixth wheels. Completely redundant," Neil teased.

"Whatever happened to that girl you were with?" Paige asked.

Neil shrugged. "Meh. She was fun while it lasted."

Liv shuddered, the memory of him throwing himself against her flashing through her mind.

"Wasn't she working on the Polar Express?" Paige pressed.

"Only for a few months. She moved back to California," Neil said flatly. "It was good timing. I don't think actresses are my thing."

"You're stupid picky," Krista said.

"Is he, though?" Liv muttered under her breath, and Jonah chuckled softly. The sleigh pulled forward, and Liv braced herself against the seat.

"What about you two?" Krista said, pointing to Paige and Jonah. Liv felt him tense next to her.

"Oh, stop," Paige said, waving her off, but it felt to Liv like she welcomed the discussion.

"No, seriously," Krista continued, "we're all friends. Why can't we talk about it?"

Liv took a breath and looked the opposite direction, pretending to be admiring the scenery.

"There's nothing to talk about," Paige brushed her off, and without turning her head, Liv could sense the group turning their eyes on Jonah.

"I'm not sure what you want me to say," he said.

"Maybe tell us why you just stopped calling or texting her back?" Krista asked, and Liv's eyes widened. There weren't many people around them, and the ones who were seemed to be engaged in their own intimate conversations, but the tension and discomfort continuing to build within her was clearly on public display. She shoved her hands deeper into her pockets and buried her chin and mouth beneath her coat collar.

Jonah didn't answer, and Neil took the opportunity to take a dig at him.

"I know how it is," he said wryly. "Too many women, too little time."

At that, Liv couldn't help herself, and a reply burst out of her. "He's not like that!"

Paige leaned forward. "No offense, but you've known him for what, a week?"

Liv nodded self-consciously.

"Yeah. We've known each other since high school."

"Leave her be," Ryan said. "Knowing each other a long time kind of makes us biased."

"Seriously?" Paige said, annoyance flaring in her tone.

"People change," Ryan shrugged.

"Not that fast," Neil smirked.

Liv mustered her courage. "It's true, I haven't known you or Jonah for long, but this whole thing," she motioned to their group, "seems toxic to me. I came today for a nice pre-Christmas sleigh ride, and instead, I'm sitting here listening to people who are supposed to be friends slam each other. This isn't how friends act, this is—"

"Liv," Jonah cut in, his voice low. "Stop."

She looked at him, her eyes flashing.

"You don't know what you're talking about," he said gently.

Liv began to shiver and was immediately transported back to Christmas Eve in New York...

· · ·

She and Connor had been dressed to the nines at a party thrown by one of his clients. Everything about that evening had seemed perfect. Liv was thrilled with the red dress she'd been wearing, her hair was pulled up into a sleek high bun, and the caterers were phenomenal. She held onto Connor's arm, following him to group after group, eventually ending up in a conversation with a potential investor and his wife.

"I'm thinking of purchasing some real estate near Destin. The market's low after the hurricane," the man had said.

"Actually, I've heard that Rosemary Beach is the best option right now—" Liv had started, excited to finally have something to contribute.

Connor cut her off with an abrasive laugh. "Liv, stop. You don't know what you're talking about..."

"...Liv?" Jonah's voice cut in, snapping her back to the present.

She looked up at him, her breathing stilted, then looked away and wiped a tear from her cheek.

"Liv," Jonah tried again, putting a hand on her arm, but she pulled away.

Her ears were ringing and she stared desperately at the trees, unable to process anything anyone else in the group was saying. She needed this to be over. Right now.

After a few painful moments, she recognized the sleigh had turned back toward the meeting point and was nearing the backside of her cottage.

"Stop!" she yelled, and the driver immediately pulled on the reins. The snow wasn't particularly deep here, and she was wearing her boots.

"I'm sorry," she said, standing and pushing past Jonah and Paige. "I'm not feeling well," she yelled to the driver. "I'm going to get off here."

"Are you sure? I could—" the driver stammered.

"No, this is great. Sorry to disrupt." She moved to the side door, opened it, and jumped to the snow before he could get up to lower the steps.

Jonah called after her, but she didn't turn to acknowledge him. Instead, she ran, immediately becoming short of breath in the high altitude air, but she didn't stop. Liv ran until she felt her lungs were going to burst and finally reached the steps to Holly Bough. Fumbling with her key, she opened the door and practically fell over the threshold. Frantically removing her boots, she locked the door and collapsed on the couch sobbing.

iv started to the sound of pounding on her door.

"Liv? It's Jonah; please open up."

She lifted herself to sitting, rubbing her puffy eyes and orienting herself. What time was it? Pulling her phone from her pocket, she saw it was a few minutes to one. The sleigh ride was at noon—had she drifted off?

"Liv!" Jonah called again. "I'm sorry, and I'd love to talk. Please open the door."

The hurt from his comment still throbbed inside her. She couldn't do that again. Be put in her place by a man who purported to care about her.

On the other hand...*that* man didn't ever come to her door to apologize afterward... She rose to her feet and walked to the door, wondering if he'd already given up. Slowly opening the front door, she found him sitting on her porch steps with his head in his hands.

"Liv," he breathed, hurrying to his feet. He took in her appearance and winced. "Can I come in for a minute?"

She nodded, retreating inside and taking a seat at the

kitchen table. Jonah closed the door behind him, took off his snowy boots, and sat across from her.

"Paige and I—we have a history."

"I've gathered," Liv said, more coldly than she'd intended.

"We've been together a couple of times—once just after high school and once—"

"Last year," Liv cut in.

Jonah nodded. "The thing you have to understand is, I get that they're not perfect. I get that Neil's a player, Paige is overbearing, Ryan is...well, he's actually a super nice guy, Krista is Paige's 'yes-man,' and all together they can be a little intense."

Liv nodded in agreement.

"They're also the only people that stuck by me during everything that happened after Oliver passed," he said, leaning his forearms on the table and sagging slightly. "I know you read the articles—"

"One article," she corrected.

"One article, then—there are others if you get bored later," he grinned but quickly sobered when Liv didn't match his smile. "You know it was bad. Everyone seemed to rally around me after the funeral, but as soon as I went downhill," he shook his head, slicing his hand through the air in front of him. "I became a liability. Paige called me up—the first person to call and invite me out to do anything since I got fired—and I know she may have had ulterior motives, but honestly? Who'd be interested in a guy who was blasted sixty percent of his waking hours and hungover the other forty?" He leaned back in his chair, crossing his arms across his chest. "Having people to spend time with was the first step in my recovery."

"I wasn't trying to attack them," Liv said softly. "I know you care about your friends, but that conversation was so awkward for me. And they were attacking your character—"

"They have every right to. They've seen me at my best and my worst. And honestly, I don't blame them for still being skeptical. I haven't even convinced myself that I'm a decent person."

Liv took a deep breath, noticing the sadness in his eyes as he spoke. "When you told me I didn't know what I was talking about—that's what Connor used to say to me. Nothing I did was right. None of my opinions were ever warranted..."

Jonah reached across the table and took her hand in his. "I'm really sorry, Liv. I didn't mean—"

"I know. It just worries me that I'm not ready—or maybe I'll always see things through that lens. The same story he drove into me over and over again. I don't want to be needy or sensitive—"

"Having sensitivities isn't a bad thing. It just means you need to find a partner who understands how to protect them."

Liv felt his hand on hers and heard the words coming out of his mouth, and her heart began to race. The relief of talking through what had happened was hitting her full-force, and he was touching her, both body and mind. She scooted her chair back and walked toward him when 'Yellow Submarine' blasted from her cellphone still on the couch.

Adjusting her trajectory, she quickly walked over to turn it off. "I'm sorry," she muttered. "I thought I had this on silent." She hastily sent Matt's call to voicemail. He could wait.

Before she could slip it into her pocket, Matt called again, buzzing this time instead of singing to her. Jonah stood and turned toward her.

"I—it's work," she smiled apologetically. "It must be urgent. Do you mind?"

Jonah nodded and walked to the cupboard next to the sink, pulled out a glass, and filled it with water.

"Hey, Matt, I'm kind of busy—"

"Liv, we have a situation," Matt said hurriedly.

"What do you mean?"

"You remember Bianca Harris?"

"Of course I do, is something wrong?"

"No, no, everything went perfectly. We completed her project three days ago, but the problem is...she wants to meet with *you* on a new idea she has for her loft."

"That doesn't sound like a situation; that's amazing!" Liv exclaimed. "That's a huge account and the fact that she wants—"

"Tomorrow, Liv. She wants to meet with you tomorrow."

"Christmas Eve?"

"She's Jewish."

Liv was speechless for a moment while she processed this. "Couldn't she meet with—"

"Tried that. She insisted. I know you understand how—"

"No, I get it," Liv sighed, her heart dropping. If she wasn't there, they could lose her loyalty. Women like Bianca weren't used to being told no. And they were absolutely used to dropping businesses like a bad habit if they didn't meet all of their expectations.

"I'll be there. What time?"

"I pushed it back as far as I could. She wanted you for breakfast, but I kindly requested a noon appointment."

"Thanks, Matt, talk soon." She hung up and took a deep breath.

"Everything okay?" Jonah asked, setting his glass of water on the counter.

"No," Liv sighed, tears already beginning to form in the corners of her eyes. Why was she crying? Because she had to now rush to the airport after a really crappy afternoon, or because her Christmas plans were dashed...her heart sank and nausea rolled over her. She was leaving. Now. There would be no point in coming back here for a day or two before returning to Florida. Her magical holiday was being cut short. And her time with Jonah—

"What's going on?" he asked, concern on his face as he walked toward her.

"I have to go," she whispered, a tear dropping to her cheek.

"What do you mean—?"

"There's a client—a big-time client in New York—who hired us to do a huge redesign of her two-story walk up, and now she wants to meet with me for another project on one of her other properties in the Upper East Side—" she paused, rubbing her forehead with her index finger. "It's non-negotiable. If I don't show for this meeting, I'd be potentially waving goodbye to a third of our income next quarter."

"Wouldn't she understand, especially over the holidays?"

Liv laughed. "You'd think so, but no. That's not how New Yorkers roll."

Jonah leaned against the counter. "So...you're leaving. Like, now?"

She nodded. "I'm going to hop on and buy a flight quickly; then I'll need to pack—"

"Can I drive you to the airport?"

"Really?"

"Yeah, of course. I want to spend as much time as I can with you."

A lump formed in Liv's throat. This was going to be goodbye. She knew it was coming eventually, but the abruptness of this shift left her reeling. It was likely she'd never see Jonah again, and even though she'd only known him for a short time, this realization filled her with dread.

"I'd love that," she choked out.

He nodded. "I can take care of cleaning out the kitchen for check-out. You go do what you need to do."

"Thank you," she said, then rushed to her room for her laptop.

21

After watching Jonah secure her bags in the covered bed of his truck, Liv jumped into the passenger seat and buckled up as Jonah headed toward Sprucewood. She'd purchased a flight that left at seven o'clock, and it was already four-fifteen. As helpful as Jonah had been with the kitchen, since she hadn't been planning to go and her belongings were strewn across the cottage, packing hadn't exactly been efficient.

Now that she was driving away, she felt a new sense of grief at leaving too soon. She'd been looking forward to spending another few days in her Hallmark worthy cottage. She'd made plans to sit by the fire and drink hot cocoa on Christmas Eve surrounded by Christmas villages and whimsical light from the tree, and now? She'd be sleeping on the couch at Sara's apartment by herself because there was no way she'd be up for going to a party with her friend after landing past midnight and arriving closer to two in the morning.

And she couldn't even think about her nixed plans with Jonah on Christmas Day. She'd never tried a fried turkey and—

"What're you thinking?" Jonah asked as he pulled onto the highway.

Liv sighed. "About a lot of things."

"Like what?"

"Like how I was really excited to spend Christmas here. Like how I really don't want to go back to New York," she said in a rush. "I think it's going to take more time before I'm not going to feel stressed about everything there."

"Do you have good friends there, at least?"

"That's...complicated," she said, raising an eyebrow, and Jonah grinned. "Most of my friends were connected to me *and* Connor. Together."

"Kind of awkward."

"Exactly. But I am staying with one friend—Sara."

Jonah nodded. Liv could sense tension in him—like he was holding something back. It was probably held over from their conflict this morning, but even rationalization couldn't take away the discomfort.

They made small-talk, covering topics that ranged from Liv's worst pedicure to Jonah's disdain for air travel. Though she laughed and participated, it was far from satisfying. Her soul longed for him to see her deeply and this sitting at the surface? It made her want to scream.

When the conversation lulled, Liv exhaled, her courage finally building enough to acknowledge in part the elephant in the cab.

"I didn't get to say goodbye to Bobby. Or enjoy my last plate of cookies."

"The fact that Bobby ranks at the same level as those cookies is impressive. I'll pass along the compliment."

Liv smacked his arm, then watched out the windshield as the spruce trees and granite rock walls along the highway gave way in an instant to shopping centers, a massive antique store, and industrial yards.

"I'm really going to miss this place," she breathed.

"I think this place is going to miss you," Jonah said softly, and Liv felt heat rise to her cheeks. She glanced Jonah's direction, but he remained maddeningly focused on the road ahead of him.

"Jonah—"

"So tell me more about your family," he said abruptly, talking over her.

Liv took a deep breath, frustrated by—and somehow equally grateful for—his question. The benefit of sitting in the passenger seat was that she could observe him as much as she wanted without it being weird, and she dove full-on into that guilty pleasure. If she couldn't have the conversation she wanted, she could at least have this. His eyelashes were even more impressive from a side angle, and his dimple...

She cleared her throat. "I think I told you about my growing up, so I don't want to bore you with more of that. Did I tell you about my sister Tamara?"

Jonah shook his head, and Liv launched into an explanation of maturing alongside a sister who was always slightly more perfect than she was. Not slightly, *much* more perfect than she was. Jonah asked questions, seeming to be genuinely interested. Which only made Liv more curious about everything he hadn't been willing to share about his own life, and she couldn't stop herself from going there.

"Can I ask about your family?" she asked hesitantly. "I know you didn't want to talk about it last time, so—"

"No, it's fine," Jonah cut in. "I'm not great at opening up, as I'm sure you've noticed."

Liv's mouth hung slightly open in shock. That was far too easy.

"I don't think you're *that* bad at it," she said, quickly recovering.

"Thanks. I think?"

"It was meant as a compliment," she laughed.

He took a deep breath before speaking. "I don't like talking about my family because...I kind of already have enough baggage, you know?"

Liv's brow furrowed. "How so?"

"I've lost a child, been divorced, I'm an alcoholic. What kind of person wants to saddle up with that resume on its own, but then I have to add family drama on top of it?"

This was more like it. "I mean, I kind of see it as all of those things made you who you are. People can go through a lot of junk or nothing at all and still end up as terrible people. If you've become a good person, then why would anyone hold that against you?"

Jonah chanced a glance in her direction. "Is that how you feel about yourself?"

Liv blanched slightly. "That's different."

"It's really not."

"If I was a good person, then I'd agree, but I'm not—"

"Says who?" Jonah scoffed.

"Says—me!" Liv blustered. "I know what goes on inside my head, and it's selfish and—and immature. A lot of the time."

"Right, so you're saying if I'm the same way, I'm not a good person?"

"No, you're not—"

"You're not inside my head, Liv."

Liv turned to look out her window. This is not how she'd envisioned their last conversation. Even though she knew her logic was left wanting, she couldn't bring herself to admit it.

"My parents got divorced when I was seven years old," Jonah said softly. "My dad was an alcoholic. I didn't ever see him again after watching him walk out of the house with his suitcase and a sack lunch my mom made for him."

"She made him a lunch?" Liv breathed, and Jonah nodded.

"My mom got her nursing degree and worked at the hospital in Golden for years. She ended up getting breast cancer when I was seventeen, then had it relapse when I was twenty-two. That time, it got the best of her."

Liv turned to him as the last of the frustration and defensiveness seeped out of her. "Jonah, I—"

"See what I mean about baggage?" he laughed derisively. "Now I'm not only the guy with the dead kid; I'm the guy with the abusive dad and dead mom."

Liv sat frozen in her seat. She didn't want to pity him. Well, she did, but she knew that's not what he wanted—no. She sat up straight, taking a deep breath. Something flared within her as she recognized thoughts steering her down the same road of insecurity and self-doubt.

"I know you don't want pity, but I'm allowed to feel sad for seven-year-old Jonah," she breathed. "And seventeen-year-old Jonah. And twenty-two-year-old Jonah," she said, her voice building in intensity. "Yes, you have baggage. Yes, that's probably going to make some things in your life more difficult. But there are people out there who are going to accept you for who you are. If you keep hiding all of that, you'll never know which ones they are."

Jonah's lips pursed, and Liv saw a sign for Denver International Airport in her peripheral vision.

"Are you one of those people?" he asked, and Liv's breath quickened.

"I think that's the best part of going through things yourself. It's easier to see and accept people," she said, pivoting.

"What airline are you on?" Jonah asked, scrutinizing the signs for the East and West Terminals.

"United."

He followed the road to the left, then took the exit for departures. "You didn't answer my question."

Liv's heart pounded. It was a simple question, but the way he asked it...

"Yes," she said, and she meant it more deeply than she was willing to admit. Somehow, in only a matter of weeks, she couldn't get him off her mind. Yes, he was incredibly handsome...and introverted enough to be maddeningly mysterious, but it was more than that. His past grounded him somehow; it made him interact with the world differently. With *her* differently. She felt seen when she was with him, like something between them had connected below the surface of their own consciousness. She more than accepted him for who he was. Her heart was tied to him.

This realization left her breathless as Jonah pulled up to the curb next to the United sign and put the truck in park. He hesitated momentarily before jumping out to retrieve her bags. Liv sat frozen in the passenger seat before forcing herself to open the door and step down to the sidewalk.

Her hands were shaking as Jonah stopped in front of her, setting her bags to the side. He gazed at her intently, then lifted his arms and pulled her into an embrace. She exhaled, closing her eyes as her head nestled between his neck and shoulder.

He held her—his chest rising and falling against hers—until her body melted into his, and she couldn't imagine being anywhere else. When he finally stepped back, she cringed at the thought of what came next. She had to take her bags and walk through the airport sliding glass doors. She had to walk away from him and likely never see him again.

His hands remained looped around her waist and he gazed at her intently before slowly moving his face closer to hers. Liv's throat grew thick, and she worked to pull air into her lungs. Her body remembered the feeling of his lips on hers.

With her heart pounding out of her chest, she closed her eyes and—

"Thank you for the ride," she said abruptly, stepping back from his warmth and gripping the handles of her bags tightly. "Merry Christmas," was all she could choke out before whipping her head toward the doors so he wouldn't see the tears beginning to stream down her cheeks.

22

Liv cried the entire way through security, riding the train to her gate, and off and on throughout the flight. It seemed as soon as she got ahold of herself, something else would remind her of him—a scruffy face, blue eyes, shaggy hair—and the flood-works would start again. She'd planned on getting work done, but she simply couldn't focus. Watching Modern Family for four hours didn't make her feel any better, but at least it was a worthy distraction. And made the sobbing somewhat socially acceptable.

She landed, collected her bags, and took an Uber into Manhattan, thankfully out of tears and unable to embarrass herself further at that point. The view out her window seemed almost surreal. She hadn't been gone long enough to justify her intense perspective shift, but everything seemed cold—dirtier than she'd remembered, even in the middle of the night—and absolutely unforgiving. The hustle and bustle of the city used to fill her with excitement, but now it felt almost sinister. Overwhelming. She was exhausted, she knew that. But still. The bright lights on each building seemed to purposefully spite her throbbing head.

Liv laid her head back on the seat and focused on the days ahead of her. She'd get a few hours sleep, meet with Bianca, spend the evening with Sara, survive Christmas dinner with Sara's friends, spend the twenty-sixth at the office with Matt wrapping up a few things, then fly home a day earlier than planned. Her parents would be thrilled, and it would go fast. Hopefully fast enough that she'd stop seeing Jonah's face everywhere she looked.

When the car pulled to a stop, she thanked the driver and trudged across the sidewalk to the front doors. She entered the code Sara had given her to the building, then wrangled her bags up a flight of stairs to Sara's apartment. As promised, the key was under the potted plant to the right of the door, and Liv seamlessly let herself in.

As discreetly as possible, she rolled her bags next to the futon Sara had set out for her in the living room and found her way to the bathroom down the hall. Not even taking the time to find her toiletries and brush her teeth, she relieved herself, washed her hands, and found her way back to the mattress where she collapsed and fell instantly to sleep.

In what felt like barely an hour, she woke to light streaming in through the balcony window and quickly checked her phone for the time. Ten-thirty. She needed to move.

After taking a quick shower and pulling her hair up into a twist, she went directly to the fridge to find something to eat. She felt slightly guilty about rummaging for food until she spotted a note from her friend on the counter that she'd missed the night before.

I won't be up early—late night! Help yourself and see you after your appointment! XO Sara

Liv poured herself a bowl of cereal with the almond milk Sara had in the fridge and snagged an apple for the road. Putting her tablet and laptop in her shoulder bag, she slipped Sara's key into her pocket and quietly left the apartment.

Liv was proud of herself. She'd succeeded in pressing on from one task to the next, barely allowing herself time to think or ruminate on emotional matters. And wasn't that exactly why she both loved and loathed New York? She was a more ruthless version of herself here. Driven. Her own task-master. But even as she patted herself on the back for being so focused, she could already feel it wasn't going to last this time. She could put on a good face for a few weeks—maybe even months—but this life...

No. She wasn't going to go there.

Though she knew the call might drop once she went underground, she decided to at least try reaching Tamara. Why she chose her sister in that moment made no sense to her logically, but there it was. They hadn't spoken since their chat the other day, and—shockingly—she actually had a desire to check-in.

"Hey!" Tamara said, answering the phone on the second ring.

"Hey, happy Christmas Eve," Liv said, smiling.

"How are you? Doing something fun, I hope?"

"Kind of? I'm meeting with a client."

"On Christmas Eve?"

"She's Jewish."

"Ah. Well, hopefully you'll be finished in time to do something fun."

"That's the goal. Are you building gingerbread houses?"

"You know it. Mom went all out this year. There's candy

rocks, miniature marshmallow trees, probably six different kinds of gummy candy."

Liv sighed. "I wish I was there."

"We're saving you a set to make when you get here."

"Thank you!" Liv exclaimed, surprised at how genuinely excited she was to participate in their childhood tradition.

"How are you doing?" Tamara asked.

"Better."

"Good. We're all excited to see you."

"Me too."

"Oh, wow. I have to run save Dad's garden from the game of tag the kids are playing. Talk soon?"

"Sounds good. Love you."

"Love you, too."

She arrived in front of Bianca's building breathing hard, but with ten minutes to spare. The subway stop had only been two blocks away, and she was thankful she didn't have to cover more ground than that in heels. Her feet had somehow already adapted to wearing flip-flops and boots, and they weren't keen on being mercilessly pinched and squeezed again.

Checking in with the doorman, Liv waited to be allowed entrance. She turned to the street and lackadaisically watched people passing by when suddenly her heart stopped. A man wearing a baseball cap caught her eye on the opposite side of the road, and for a split second, she thought it was him. It wasn't—that would be utterly impossible. Jonah didn't fly. She didn't even know if he did road trips or any other travel that didn't include 'hurtling through space in a metal canister,' as he'd put it. A laugh escaped her lips as she remembered his brief but impassioned rant on the drive to the airport.

"Miss?" she heard a voice call behind her.

"Hmm?"

The doorman walked around his desk and opened the door for her with his gloved hand.

"Thank you."

She entered the elevator that had already been pre-programmed for the correct floor and waited while it ascended. When it dinged, she stepped off into a marble hallway. Light streamed through an open window to her right, illuminating the enormous solid wood door that stood magnificently before her.

Liv raised her fist to knock, but the door swung open before her knuckles made contact. Bianca greeted her with an elated smile. She wore a mink around her neck and her emerald green gown fell to the floor, swishing along the tile as she beckoned Liv into the apartment.

"What a lovely day, isn't it?" Bianca said, picking up her dwarf Pomeranian and kissing its head affectionately. "I know it's a holiday for you tomorrow, so I'll make this fast..."

Liv followed her around between the rooms, furiously scribbling notes and making suggestions when warranted. Bianca had a sense of design that was all her own, and Liv had learned on their first project that clarification was key. Bianca didn't want someone to tell her how to design her space; she wanted someone to make her colorful imagination a reality.

Liv sketched a sample floor plan with walls knocked out, walls put up, and even an addition that included purchasing the unit above and next door. When Liv left four hours later, she felt like slumping to the ground outside Bianca's door. And she likely would've had the marble tile been warmer. She would definitely need that time with Matt on the twenty-sixth to hammer out drafts, but for now, she could go home and recover.

Stepping out onto the street, Liv walked back to the subway station. She descended the stairs, going into autopilot. Her transportation pass was still active, but as she bypassed the payment terminals and followed the crowd through the turnstiles toward the train that would take her back to Sara's, she slowed. Someone promptly ran into her back and shouted a serious of expletives at her as they passed, and she hastily moved out of the stream of people. It was almost four-thirty, which meant Sara would be leaving for her party in only a couple of hours. But it was Christmas Eve, and nothing about this felt like Christmas.

The buildings upstairs were decked out with lights, wreaths, and objects that were supposed to fill the beholder with Christmas cheer, but all of it—the smells, the sounds— only reminded her of disappointment. Of walking quickly behind Connor as he stress-walked to a party, of adjusting her dress over and over again so he'd hopefully pay her a compliment, of wasting *so many Christmas Eves* trying to be his trophy wife and always failing. She wanted Sprucewood. She wanted the quiet, down-home Christmas celebration she'd been exposed to. She wanted to fry a dang turkey.

As people flowed through the tunnel next to her, she made a snap decision. She wasn't going to head back to the apartment until she did the one thing she'd always wanted to do on Christmas Eve in New York. It was cheesy, yes— Connor had been right about that—but she didn't care. If she couldn't have Sprucewood, she at least wanted to drink apple cider while window shopping in Times Square. And actually admire the Christmas tree at Rockefeller Center instead of rushing past it.

She texted Sara, apologizing for the change of plans—but promising she'd see her the next day—then boarded her train.

23

When she surfaced to the street, the city was nearly dark, and the lights of Times Square buzzed around her. After a good night's sleep, the busyness was less formidable, but it still felt unnatural after her time at the Cottages. Liv had always envisioned herself working her way into the upper-crust of Manhattan, but now...she longed to be back amongst the trees. *With Jonah*, her mind asserted, but she forcefully pushed the thought away.

Tucking her hands in her coat pocket, she rounded the corner and walked toward Rockefeller Center. Her feet were already aching—stupid heels—and the air felt significantly colder here than in Colorado; it chilled her to the bone. Walking quickly, it took only minutes to reach her destination, and she stopped in awe. It was like she'd suddenly been transported into a wonderland. The tree was exponentially more prominent than she'd remembered. She began walking closer as if drawn to it like a bug to a flame.

"Liv?" a voice called behind her.

She stopped in her tracks, and her blood ran cold.

"Liv, is that you?" Connor said, walking briskly toward her, towing a woman wearing a red beret against her jet black hair on his arm. She looked even younger in person.

"Hey," he said, flashing an arrogant smile and adjusting his abhorrent glasses. "What are you doing here?"

She forced her mouth to move. "I'm taking in the sights."

"Christmas Eve," he chuckled, nudging his fiancé. "What better way to spend it, right?"

Bile rose in Liv's throat, and she swallowed hard. "Have you met Aliyah?" he asked, knowing full well she hadn't. She bit down on her tongue to keep from lashing out.

"No, I don't think we've been introduced," Liv said after taking a breath.

The woman smiled and extended a hand.

"I'm Liv."

"Oh," Aliyah said, realization dawning on her face. "You're Connor's—"

"Yep," Liv cut her off, rocking on her feet. "Are you two off to a party tonight?"

"No," Connor laughed. "We wanted to spend the night, just the two of us."

"Of course you did," Liv muttered, but then forced a smile to her face. "Who wouldn't?"

"Are you—" Connor motioned to the space next to her, "—alone? I mean, by yourself for Christmas?"

Liv's cheeks grew hot. Connor waited, his eyes boring into hers as if challenging her to be good enough. To be worthy.

"I—"

"There you are," a man's voice said next to her, and Liv snapped her head toward the sound involuntarily.

"I step away to get cider and you disappear on me," he said, his voice upbeat, but his eyes told a different story. An intensity burned there, and Liv couldn't look away. He wasn't wearing a hat, and his regular flannel button-up had been replaced with a crew neck sweater, wool coat, and a scarf around his neck. Liv was speechless.

Jonah set their steaming cups on the ledge behind her and wrapped an arm around her waist, gently kissing her cheek. Her skin tingled, and she could barely remain upright.

"Who's this?" he asked, turning toward the couple in front of him.

"I'm Connor, and this is my fiancé, Aliyah."

"Ah," Jonah said, keeping his free hand in his pocket. "Nice glasses."

Liv stifled a laugh, pretending to cough into her elbow.

"Thanks," Connor said, looking uncomfortably between Jonah and Liv.

"This is Jonah," Liv explained, unable to keep the giddy smile off her face. Jonah was here. In New York. How was he here!? Why was he here? And how—

"Are you two—" Connor started, pointing again, but this time motioning back and forth between them. If he didn't stop with the patronizing hand motions, Liv was going to literally punch him in the face. And hopefully break his ironic frames.

"Very much so," Jonah said, his voice low. He pulled her closer and stood to his full height, at least a head taller than Connor. Liv's thoughts swirled, and she took a deep breath to steady herself.

"Huh," Connor said, raising an eyebrow as he scrutinized Jonah's face. "Well, it's great seeing you, Liv. Looks like...you're doing well."

"Good luck with the wedding," Liv said, looking pointedly at his fiancé.

"Nice to meet you," Aliyah said uncomfortably.

Connor tugged on his wife-to-be's arm as he sauntered off in the direction of the skating rink.

Liv stood in complete shock, feeling Jonah's arm still

holding her tightly, but not fully allowing herself to believe it was real.

"He's a tool," Jonah said, and Liv twisted her body toward him, pulling his face desperately toward her with both hands. She explored his stubbly cheeks as his lips crushed against hers. Jonah wrapped both arms easily around her waist as her knees went weak, lifting her slightly from the concrete and pressing her body tightly against his. She felt the warmth in his lips, and the chilled tip of his nose on her cheek as her hands brushed his jaw and played in his hair. The chatter, music, and car horns seemed to fade away entirely as she lost herself in his touch.

Separating slightly, she gasped for breath, her heart pounding frantically with his face an inch from her own.

"Hi," he teased, his voice husky.

"Hi."

His lips brushed hers as he lowered her fully to the ground, his arms still tied around her.

"How—when—" Liv said, attempting to form a coherent sentence as she looked up into his eyes. "You hate planes—and I'm—" she took a deep breath. "How are you here!?"

Jonah exhaled, grinning mischievously with his dimple in full view. "I do hate flying. It was horrific."

"Then why—"

He pressed a finger to her lips. "After you left, I—" he paused, searching for the right words. "I couldn't stop thinking about you. I know that sounds crazy. I've been telling myself I'm crazy, and maybe I am, but Liv. I haven't felt like this—ever."

Liv's eyes were riveted on his, begging him to continue. She hadn't had someone talk to her like this. Ever.

"Loneliness has become a way of life for me," he went on, "and since I met you—it feels like you see something in me, like we understand each other in some weird way? I don't know how to describe it. And we've only known each other for what, two weeks?"

"Not even," Liv smiled.

"Right. Crazy, like I said. But I drove home after dropping you at the airport, and I couldn't sit down. It was like I was missing something. Like you'd started to fill a space in me—not that it's your job to fix me, that's not it—but I—"

Liv lifted herself on her toes and kissed him lightly. "I haven't heard you talk this much ever."

Jonah shrugged, reaching up and holding her hand to his heart. "I bought a red-eye ticket."

"How did you find me?"

"I remembered your business name, and I looked it up, then realized halfway there that it definitely wouldn't be open. I panicked slightly and wondered if I was going to have to text you, but then there's that sign on the door—"

"With Matt's number," Liv grinned. "You talked to Matt?"

"Nice guy."

"And he gave you Sara's number," Liv said, piecing things together.

Jonah nodded. "She said you were headed here. And that you loved apple cider."

Liv grinned. "The timing couldn't have been better, you know."

"I thoroughly enjoyed playing your boyfriend."

"Playing?"

Jonah smiled, closing the space between them.

24

"How was sleeping on the floor?" Sara yawned, finally stumbling out of her bedroom at one o'clock in the afternoon.

"I've definitely had worse nights," Jonah smiled. "Thanks for letting me crash."

"I offered for him to take the futon since he had to sleep on the plane last night," Liv said. "He insisted."

"Quite the gentleman," Sara teased, pulling her hair up into a high ponytail. "I feel awful."

"I made you eggs," Liv said, sliding a plate toward the opposite side of the counter. "You might need to heat them up."

Sara picked up the plate gratefully.

"How was the party?" Liv asked.

"Food was great, company? So-so," Sara grinned.

"Matt was there?"

"He was. He asked about *you*," Sara said, pointing at Jonah.

"What'd you tell him?" Jonah asked, grinning.

Liv couldn't stop staring at the way his mouth moved—his

hands as they ran through his hair, the way his jeans fit, his broad shoulders—and her heart fluttered uncontrollably every time that dimple appeared in his cheek.

Sara laughed. "Well, since I talked with you for all of five minutes, I of course told him your entire life history."

"Perfect," Jonah laughed.

"Are you two coming to Christmas dinner?" Sara asked, pulling her newly warmed plate from the microwave.

"I—I don't know," Liv said, turning to Jonah. "We haven't really talked about it."

Jonah leaned on the counter. "I promised Liv a great Christmas dinner, but I don't think I'm going to be able to make good on that."

"The food's going to be top-notch," Sara cajoled. "The only cost is making small-talk with people you don't know," she grinned, putting a forkful of eggs into her mouth.

"Seems pretty steep," Jonah teased.

Liv grinned. "I'll do all the talking. You can just stand next to me and look pretty."

"Deal."

Liv walked toward him and looped her arms around his waist. "I'm really glad you're here."

"Ugh!" Sara groaned. "Get a room."

"Are you offering yours?" Liv teased.

"Never-mind, go on the balcony," she said, feigning disgust.

Jonah stepped backward, pulling Liv toward the back door.

"Seriously? I was kidding! It's cold out there," Sara warned.

Liv laughed, following Jonah out onto the cold wood in her bare feet, sliding the door closed behind her. He kissed her gently, brushing her hair away from her face.

She snuggled close to him, shivering in the cold morning air. "This is the best Christmas ever," she breathed.

"Agreed."

"Jonah..." she hesitated, and Jonah pulled back, inspecting her face. "I don't want to put a damper on anything, but it really hurt to leave you in Sprucewood. I know we're together now, and I should be able to just focus on that, but...I'm already dreading the moment we have to say goodbye again."

He nodded, looking out onto the side street below them.

"Where do we go from here?" Liv asked.

"I don't know," he admitted. "I didn't think past getting to you."

"I've never done the long-distance thing. Successfully," she said, and Jonah turned his attention back to her.

"I'm at a point in my life where I'm fairly flexible," he said.

"But your house—"

"Liv, my house is empty. Yes, it's paid for, but I don't have a life there."

"Wait, how did you get out of maintenance duty? Aren't you supposed to be—"

"Neil's covering for me."

Liv raised an eyebrow.

"I know. Poor decision-making skills, misogynistic, but fairly good at fixing things in a pinch. And mostly a good friend."

"How long is your work contract for?"

"At the Cottages? Until the end of February."

Liv nodded, processing this information. "Two months."

"Two months."

"Have you ever been to Florida? My dad is always looking for good help."

"I haven't committed to any summer gigs yet," Jonah said.

"It's not like I have to be in Florida to work, I can pretty much work anywhere."

"We have good wifi in Sprucewood. And an empty house."

Liv's heart hammered so loud in her ears that she could barely think straight. "Are we going to actually try this?"

"I'm game if you are."

"What if we get sick of each other."

"It happens," Jonah said softly, gently brushing his lips against hers.

"What if we hurt each other."

"It happens," he shrugged, holding his kiss longer this time, and Liv slipped her cold hands underneath the back of his shirt.

"What if—"

"We'll figure it out, Liv," he said, breathing her in. "You and me, we're survivors."

"It's a little scary," she whispered, her body beginning to shiver.

"Everything worth doing is."

She let her fears slip away as he kissed her. She could be nervous. And elated. And terrified, all at once. Because this Liv didn't let opportunities pass her by. This Liv—for once —*knew what she wanted*. And right now. On this freezing platform. With this man. She wanted to leap.

THE END

ALSO BY CINDY GUNDERSON

Tier Trilogy (Tier 1, Tier 2, Tier 3)

I Can't Remember

Let's Try This Again, But This Time in Paris

Yes, And

The New Year's Party

www.CindyGunderson.com

Instagram: @CindyGWrites

Facebook: @CindyGWrites

ABOUT THE AUTHOR

Cindy is first and foremost mother to her four beautiful children and wife to her charming and handsome husband, Scott. She is a musician, a homeschooler, a gardener, an athlete, an actor, a lover of Canadian chocolate, and most recently, a writer.

Cindy grew up in Airdrie, AB, Canada, but has lived most of her adult life between California and Colorado. She currently resides in the Denver metro area. Cindy graduated from Brigham Young University in 2005 with a B.S. in Psychology, minoring in Business. She serves actively within her church and community and is always up for a new adventure.

Made in the USA
Columbia, SC
09 December 2021